A TENDER KISS

The temperature changed, and a cool breeze caressed her cheek. She looked down. The grass was gone, in its place were the feet of a woman in strappy sandals. In the distance she could see Merry, who blew her a kiss goodbye. Sydney reached out to stop her, but the kiss slid up her fingertips, over her hand and arm, before claiming her whole body in a warm embrace. Sydney lowered her hand, satisfied.

Warmth surrounded her, and she reached out and felt a man's jacket slide over her arms. She knew it was a man's because of the alluring aroma of aftershave and cologne. She welcomed the comfort and looked up at the generous stranger.

Drew looked down at her. With a deliberateness that belied his strength, he took her into his arms.

When her head was resting in the bend of his arm, his right hand wrapped around her waist, and he bent his head and claimed her mouth in a kiss so tender, if it hadn't been so sweet it would have broken her heart.

They were adversaries. Enemies. But his kiss took her to a dimension where there was only pleasure. He groaned with wanting, and she enticed him by making her body meet his.

His mouth brushed hers, bringing Sydney up on her toes.

Flirt

Carmen Green

KENSINGTON PUBLISHING CORP.
http://www.kensingtonbooks.com

DAFINA BOOKS are published by

Kensington Publishing Corp.
850 Third Avenue
New York, NY 10022

All Kensington titles, imprints and distributed lines are available at special quantity discounts for bulk purchases for sales promotion, premiums, fund-raising, educational or institutional use.

Special book excerpts or customized printings can also be created to fit specific needs. For details, write or phone the office of the Kensington Special Sales Manager: Kensington Publishing Corp., 850 Third Avenue, New York, NY 10022. Attn. Special Sales Department. Phone: 1-800-221-2647.

First Printing: October 2005
10 9 8 7 6 5 4 3 2 1

Printed in the United States of America

Acknowledgments

Thank you Tina Green for your love and the corniest book titles ever, and thank you to Jennifer St. Giles for giving me the ending of this story. You're amazing.

1

Sydney Morris sat outside FLIRT, the women's novelty store her mother had owned until her death two weeks ago, and wondered why she was here.

The store looked like a dull penny in the daylight, worn and washed free of color and life. She picked at the steering wheel with her thumb and hated what her mother was trying to do. They'd never had anything in common. Had not spoken in more than twenty years. Sydney had barely seen her, except for the occasional blip on the TV screen when Merry Morris was getting sued again by some group that found her stores too objectionable for their upstanding community. But that hadn't stopped Merry from interjecting herself into their neighborhoods, and now into her estranged daughter's life. From the grave.

How appropriate.

"I don't want her store. Sell it and the contents to the first taker."

Lori King, her mother's attorney, looked up at her with sorrow dripping from her eyes. Sydney didn't consider herself to be an emotional person, but Lori's look sank into her and wouldn't let go. She felt compelled to tell the woman she was wasting her energy, but didn't.

"I know you don't want to hear this, but you're the spitting image of Merry."

The comment threw Sydney. Here was another person who knew her mother better than she. After twenty years, her mother's ability to hurt her was still there. "You're right. I don't want to hear it."

Lori seemed to struggle with her next words, making Sydney wonder if Lori and Merry had been close friends.

Had they shared intimate details of their lives? Had Lori counseled Merry to invite the daughter she'd abandoned back into her life?

Sydney brushed her shoulder-length hair from her eyes, looking at the structure that had been so important to her mother. The place was trashy looking, and the bleak January gray sky didn't make it better.

"I don't want it."

"I'll follow your wishes, but there are things you need to know. Let's go inside."

"No."

"Stubborn, too," Lori said and shook her head. "Many years ago, when your mother was told by the male community leaders to get out, her spine would straighten just like yours, and she wouldn't back down. By day the hypocrites vilified her, but by night they begged to be in her bed. Merry was a fighter. She retaliated against the two-faced bastards by selling their wives vibrators with rechargeable batteries."

The lawyer laughed. "Oh, how we celebrated when the *Rabbit* became Merry's number one best-seller. The resemblance between you two is striking."

Sydney walked away from the limousine Lori had arrived in and went back to her car. This stroll down memory lane wasn't her idea of the most popular way to spend her lunch hour.

"I have no desire to see the inside of that store. I have no desire to abide by a single one of Merry's wishes. No offense, ma'am, but I have no desire to know anyone that associated with my mother."

"How much do you earn as a bookkeeper, Ms. Morris?"

"That's none of your business." Sydney confronted the woman, ignoring the cold wind that rippled through the parking lot. "Get out of my life, Ms. King."

"Your mother has willed you her store worth three-quarters of a million dollars."

Although shocked disbelief went through her like fire, Sydney hid her surprise. This was some type of stupid game, and she wasn't going to participate. "I don't believe you."

"It's got to be hard sitting in that two-man office all day long, all alone, making twenty-three thousand dollars a year. How long before you earn a million dollars, forty years? Can you wait that long to realize your dreams?"

"What I dream about is my business."

Lori's voice softened. "Wouldn't it be nice to realize some of those dreams now? Why won't you at least open your mind and consider the offer?"

"I find it strange that I haven't seen or heard from

her in a lifetime, but now she wants to give me something. No, I refuse to be sucked into this . . . drama."

"Would your father object?"

"Leave him out of this. She didn't want us, and we don't need her."

"Stop being the hero for a moment and listen." Lori's voice took on an edge, and Sydney met her icy gaze.

"This is *your* store. *Your* property. *Your* problem, if that's what you want to think. By law you *have* to do something. What that is is up to you. Your mother cared about you. Despite everything."

"Don't defend her. I was raised by my father because my mother decided she wanted to live in the world and not at home with us."

"Why are you so sure you're right? What happens if one day you find out that what you believed or were told was fact wasn't? Is your heart so cold that you can't even give her the benefit of the doubt?"

Sydney had often asked herself the same question; then someone told her that a person's actions spoke louder than any words they could say. If Merry had wanted to present her side of the story, she'd had every day since Sydney had turned eighteen to do so. Sydney hadn't realized she'd been waiting to hear from her mother until several years had passed. Then she buried that hope long before Merry's passing.

"Merry never reached out to me. I'll be fine without her money or her sentiment."

"Don't you deserve to make your dreams come true now? Being the owner of FLIRT could change everything. Just imagine a life where you have choices."

"I don't mean to be rude, Ms. King, but I have no interest in owning a sex-toy store! I could use the money, and since I have to do something, I will." Sydney opened the door of her Hyundai. "Sell the property."

The cold wind battered Lori's face, but she didn't react. Dread filled Sydney's stomach. "What?"

"If you sell now, you get nothing."

"Is this some kind of game?" Sydney looked at the sky, shaking her head.

"The deal is that you have to work in and manage FLIRT, and make it profitable for six months, and if you do, you'll receive an inheritance worth seven hundred fifty thousand dollars. If you don't, you get nothing. You have forty-eight hours to decide. And, Sydney?"

"Yes?"

"Everything we've talked about is strictly confidential."

Lori walked to the limousine and slipped inside. The car pulled away.

Sydney stood with her hands folded in front of her, her chin on her chest.

Why was this happening to her? Sydney had acknowledged the feelings of loss when Merry had died two weeks ago, but now Syd wondered. Why was Merry reaching out to her now?

Another searing wind froze her lungs, and she hopped into the Hyundai and started the engine. Cranking the heater on her feet and face, she sat there, numb.

Earlier she'd been angry at being summoned here, but now Sydney was confused over the decisions she was being forced to make. Pulling off the driveway and onto the street, she dialed her cell phone, hoping her best friend would answer.

"Syd, how'd it go? Are you okay? What happened?"

The lights on the train tracks in front of her blinked, and the arm came down. Sydney lined up for the three-minute train, put her car in park and leaned back into the seat.

"Evette, catch your breath. I'm fine, and she left me her store." Relief at Evette's familiar voice filled her with comfort after the strange morning she'd had.

Where Sydney was medium height, Evette was tall, nearly six feet of legs. But she had the softest, most honest heart of any person Sydney had ever known. They'd been friends since childhood, and Sydney didn't know how she'd have survived the trials in her life without Evette. "She left me FLIRT, her adult toy store."

Evette snorted. "To do what with?"

She remembered Lori's warning. "To run or I can dispose of it."

"What are you going to do?"

"I don't know, 'Vette. There's a lot of confidential stuff tied into this situation, so I can't say too much, but I have a lot to lose if I sell."

"Then do the opposite. What's the worst possible thing that could happen?"

"Are you kidding? These are sex toys! Me, never-rock-the-boat Sydney Morris selling sex toys? I'm embarrassed just talking to you about them."

"Why? Most women have at least one vibrator."

"I don't!"

"And you should, but that's not the subject. Syd, you hate your job. You hate working with those two geeks, and what happens if you don't take the opportunity?

Your life stays the same. And that's okay, but what's wrong with change?"

Evette spoke a truth Sydney had been struggling with for several years. Her life was one boring day after the next.

"If I manage the store, I'd have to quit my job."

"All the more reason to do it. You can get a mediocre job in any city in the world. What's really holding you back? Your father?"

The end of the train blew by, rocking her small car. Finally the bar lifted, and Sydney drove over the tracks. "'Vette, I can't do this to him. He'd be so hurt. No. I'm not going to run her store."

"Syd, why did you bother to move out of his house if you were still going to operate under your father's rules?"

"What?"

"I know you're getting pissed, but he isn't in charge of your life now. That whole my-word-is-my-bond crap went out of style with platform shoes. I think you need to live your life and let him live his."

"He's the only parent I've ever known. I don't want to do anything to hurt him."

"But it's okay for him to hurt you by not allowing you to have an ounce of fun as a kid? You weren't stifled in that sterile environment? Yes, you were. I'm not criticizing—"

"It sounds like it to me."

"Syd, do what you want, but if you don't give this opportunity a chance, in fifty years when we talk about this, I don't want to hear about what you should have

13

done. Life is for the living. It doesn't get better unless you put effort into it. Look, I gotta go."

"Wait, 'Vette. Don't go yet."

"Look, I'm sorry I'm trippin' on you," Evette said, sounding stressed. "This business with these athletes and the coed orgy is getting to me. I don't know why people think PR executives are miracle workers."

Syd chuckled. "No problem and thank you."

"For what," Evette said.

"Oh, for the last thirty years of friendship." Sydney felt herself wanting to weep and shook it off. "I don't know what I'm going to do, but you've helped me focus."

"If you're smart, you'll accept this challenge and learn who you really are. Expect no less than the very best from yourself, and you'll never fail. Bye."

Syd drove through the streets, the words wrapping like a scroll through her mind. What did she have to lose? She didn't have to know Merry or even like her. But this was in essence a lottery ticket that had been blown into her lap. How could she walk away?

Sydney found herself in front of her father's house. She couldn't.

2

Outside the entryway of his new business, Drew Crawford didn't let the biting wind that seemed out of place in the heart of Georgia ruin the moment. Satisfaction was now his.

He looked at the mortar structure that represented his life savings along with money from several silent investors, and a thrill danced through him.

He was fortunate to have lived long enough to see two of his dreams come true.

A lot of guys in the bureau hadn't made it that far.

The wind escalated, and he headed toward the door, his leg aching just enough to remind him of why he'd retired.

The keys felt good in his hand, and he turned them over once, then twice, before inserting them into the lock. He pushed the door open.

"Surprise!"

Everybody that meant the world to him was gathered, smiling, hope on their faces that they'd achieved the unthinkable. He grabbed his chest, giving his best imitation stagger. "I can't believe it. This is such a surprise."

His mother and father, brothers, cousins and their wives, all stood around in full party mode. They cheered and rushed him with affection and love.

Music cranked from the restaurant sound system, reminding him to have the speakers rewired. But it felt good to be there. Right, in a way he'd always wanted but could never claim before.

He still found it hard to believe he could be his real self and not the dense cousin the family had felt they couldn't rely on.

Getting shot had probably been the best thing for him.

Drew knew that as well as he knew that the restaurant would be a success. The décor was black and gold, with tables in rows that ended in a large circle. There was also a room for private parties on the main floor, and three private dining rooms that were elevated for those couples willing to pay for the attention of a personal waiter and exclusive service. Satisfaction was everything he'd hoped it would be, including the location.

Knowing that he'd done everything right brought a big smile to his face.

This party was perfect.

Drew dropped his briefcase and shrugged out of his coat.

"Where's my glass?" he asked. "I thought this was a party?"

He accepted more hugs and kisses before settling down in a booth with a flute of champagne and the best stuffed mushrooms he'd ever tasted.

Roseanne, his sixty-seven-year-old mother, walked over with a plate of appetizers that were family favorites. "Son, I hope you have the food of love on your menu."

"Mom, I don't want people making babies in the parking lot of my restaurant. No aphrodisiac foods."

Drew smiled as his father came and engaged his bride of forty-five years in an intimate kiss. His parents weren't shy about their feelings for each other.

When his mother resurfaced, she tweaked her son's ear.

"I predict Satisfaction will be a magnificent success. But if you want it to take off right away, take your mother's advice. Lovers spend money on things that make them *feel*. Serve my mushrooms. Serve my oysters. Serve my vanilla coconut pie. If they *feel* the passion, they will come back again and again."

His cousin and biggest investor, Mike Crawford, landed in the seat across from him, a magnum of champagne in his hand.

"Tell my single son something, Michael. You and your bride still have the passion, right?"

His cousin had the grace to look embarrassed. "Yes, Aunt Rosie, but let's not talk about sex today. I haven't recovered from the last conversation we had at my bachelor party."

Everyone laughed, including Drew. His mother grabbed her husband's hand and pulled him toward the newly created dance floor.

"Watch and learn." Drew's father snuggled up to hi wife, and they twisted to their own beat.

Drew and Mike watched for a moment until Drew re alized Mike's eyes were on his wife Terra and the two littl girls they'd been trying to adopt. Terra glowed. Mother hood agreed with her. And his cousin, too. But Drew wondered how they were handling the fact that they'(never be able to have children of their own.

The thought surprised Drew. When he'd been work ing full-time for the bureau, he'd never wondered such things. His life had been consumed with catching the next bad guy. Now that he had more personal time than he'd ever imagined, his thoughts gravitated to the per sonal lives of his family. And the lack of his own.

"How's it going with the girls?" he asked.

"Terra's happy, and that makes me happy." Mik turned to him. "I love her more every day. And those girls." Mike sighed a happy sound. "They're ours. We jus have to get through the last hurdle of the adoption process. Her sister doesn't want them. Love of the streets man." He shook his head. "Can't have it both ways."

Drew had seen it too often. Children of the selfish had it worse than children of addicts. Their hurt was in visible and didn't carry the penalty of a crime.

"Terra's got a big heart," Drew said, and held out his flute for a refill. "Especially to take your behind in."

Mike laughed. "I'm back at work full-time."

"What's it been, a year?"

"Yeah, but I needed it. *We* did. Terra finished her de gree, and I loved making love to her every day. Bu enough about us." He leaned in. "I don't know how you managed to fool the family all those years you gallivanted across the globe pretending to be an idiot savant. I knew something was up with you."

"Some don't believe it was an act. I see the way Jade looks at me."

Drew's bounty hunter cousin-in-law could invoke fear in the worst criminal. Although she'd just had a baby six months ago, he had it on good authority she'd captured two of the FBI's most wanted last week. She was a legend on the streets of Atlanta. She was a weapons expert and a black belt in tae kwon do, but when she was with her baby Jada, she was transformed into a beautiful woman.

"Jade scares *me*," Mike confessed, "but you were surprised when you walked in. I saw it."

"That'd never happen, but it was a good try. I'm just glad I'm here. It took a year, but now we're just a few weeks away from this new—"

Drew stopped himself. He was never sentimental. Never reflective, except about work. Quitting the bureau had softened him in some ways, and he would allow those strange feelings to go only so far.

"What's happening with the sex store next door?"

"Closed for good. I'm thinking of buying it and turning it into an outside grill/café. I think that would attract a different kind of crowd and be very successful."

Mike tossed the idea around, his analytical mind working until a slow nod confirmed his approval. "That's a fresh idea. I like it." He tapped the side of his glass until he had everyone's attention.

"For twenty years Drew has led a colored and storied past few of us could ever imagine. But he's home now, and he's opening a restaurant that's going to be the hottest thing to hit Atlanta since the Braves won the World Series. He's going to need our support, and our money." The family laughed, and Drew hung his head, smiling. "But mostly he's going to need our love. So we'll start tonight by toasting Drew for bringing something positive to the family. To Drew, and to the success of Satisfaction."

Drew drank from his glass. He would bid on the property next door tomorrow and start phase two in six months.

Nothing could steal his joy. Nothing.

3

Sydney sat across from her father in silence, the chewing of pot roast the only movement in the quiet kitchen. Her father had never allowed much talk to interfere with mealtime, reserving after-the-dishes conversation for discussion of current events. Lenny Morris was very much a formal man. A man who took pleasure in his life being governed by rules and regulations. He cut his roasted red potatoes into quarters, added a bit of gravy to one, then put it into his mouth. He chewed twenty times, ten on the right, ten on the left. Every meal, every day.

Sydney wanted to scream.

Just once she wanted him to chew five times, then guzzle a glass of water. In his robe.

But not her father. He had a certain ideology for the world. Everything in its place. A place for everything. And those that didn't agree had no idea of the beauty of real order.

"The attorney said it would only be for six months," Sydney informed him. "Then the money would be mine."

"How much money are we talking? A few thousand? You have that much in your savings, right?"

"Of course, Dad." Ten thousand, four hundred, sixty-four dollars and seventeen cents. If he knew it was below his standard minimum of twenty thousand dollars, he'd freak out. So Sydney didn't tell him she gave money every month to sponsor thirty kids she'd heard about on TV.

"It doesn't matter; you're not doing it. I've provided a good life for you. You have a respectable job and a little house that's not fancy, but perfect for you, so why do you need that money? You don't need anything she's offering." Her father ate and chewed again.

The grandfather clock that had been a staple in their living room for as long as Sydney could remember chimed six times.

"It's too much money to walk away from," she said into the silence.

"Sydney M. Morris," he practically shouted. "I said no." Her father huffed, his maintenance uniform shirt from Georgia Tech flapping as it probably never had before. "Now let's finish eating before we have to reheat our dinner."

Sydney left her father's house an hour later, colder inside her body than the chilly temperature outside her little beige car.

She directed her car through the streets of Atlanta, driving the five miles from her father's house to her cottage-style home. By rote, she gathered her purse and the shopping bag full of clothes that were on the seat next to her.

Sydney let the handles go. The clothes were to be donated. She'd put them in the car this morning and hadn't taken them to the charity drop-off at the church.

Sydney M—

She stopped the silent chiding, her father's inability to even say her whole name, Sydney Merry Morris, making her chest ache. What pain had Merry inflicted upon her husband that he couldn't even speak her name aloud? Sydney didn't know, and her father wouldn't ever tell her.

As she dragged herself into the house via the one-car garage, the weight of indecision rested heavily upon her shoulders.

She moved the woven rug by the back hall door with her toe and wished it matched the handmade curtains she'd just put up in the tiny den/living room.

Seven hundred fifty thousand dollars.

That could buy a lot of matching rugs.

Sydney ignored her treadmill and put on her workout clothes and boxing gloves. She entered the garage and lifted the door, before wheeling out a freestanding punching bag. Adopting her fight stance, she started with slow jabs with her strong hand. Extend, pull back. Extend, pull back. She found a rhythm, increasing her accuracy and speed.

Merry hadn't contacted her for nearly twenty years. But for some reason Lori had known a lot about Sydney. That information had to have come from Merry. Why, though? It's not like they didn't live in the same area. Sydney hadn't moved or changed her name. So why now?

Because there was no fear of rejection.

Sydney punched the bag, the answer as impression able as her glove print in the leather.

Fourth amendment rights champion, sex-toy store owner Merry Morris was afraid her daughter would reject her.

Sydney followed up several jabs with a combination then stopped.

Merry would have been right.

Feeling the burn, Sydney let her arms drop to her sides, taking deep breaths.

In death, Merry had reached out to her, unable to speak for herself. Yet, Merry wanted and had gotten Sydney's attention.

Sydney walked into the house and unlaced her gloves.

She remembered the mother she once knew as a fun, loving, happy person who liked to dance around the living room with her little girl on her feet.

An involuntary twitch in her cheek spoke volumes. She'd wanted to smile at the memory, but couldn't. She wanted to know about the mother she'd once loved with childish adoration. And this was her chance.

Sydney dropped the gloves into a basket and stored it in the cabinet. Going to her purse, she pulled out Lori King's card and dialed the number.

"King."

"Ms. King, this is Sydney Morris."

Her breath drew in slowly. "Hello, Sydney. How can I help you?"

"I'd like to visit FLIRT again. This time go inside."

"I'm sorry, but I can't waste my time on a field trip. I have to have your decision. That will dictate our next move. Do you want to pursue the inheritance your mother left for you or not?"

The silence was deafening. Sydney hadn't expected an ultimatum. The good, obedient girl in her said no, but the woman who'd never taken a chance at anything answered aloud. "Yes."

"Good," Lori King said softly. She sounded relieved. "I can meet you at my office at ten A.M. tomorrow morning."

"That soon?"

"You want to get started ASAP, trust me. Paperwork has to be filed by tomorrow afternoon." She hesitated. "You should know, this isn't for the faint at heart. You can't back out once you're in."

"I have no intentions on backing out. I honor my commitments."

Sydney hadn't meant to sound self-righteous, but she couldn't take the words back.

"I'm glad to hear you're in for the long haul. Good evening."

"Bye." The dial tone hummed in her ear. Sydney could have been insulted that Ms. King had ended the call so abruptly, but hearing the dial tone made her physically sick. She ran to the bathroom and got rid of the small amount of pot roast she'd eaten.

She'd just jumped from the flower bed over a cliff.

4

Sydney sat outside FLIRT waiting for Lori. They'd signed the papers an hour ago, and Lori had given her a folder full of information she was supposed to read. She opened a bulky envelope first and palmed a handful of keys.

Going back to the folder, she flipped through, and her fingers seemed to suffer a jolt at the picture of Merry Morris smiling in all her beautiful glory.

Sydney swallowed, wishing for water.

Her mother had been a beautiful lady.

The shock of seeing Merry after all these years disturbed the foundation of Sydney's beliefs. She'd wanted to believe her mother had been a mean woman. But after talking to her father, Sydney now believed there could be more to the story.

She looked at the pocked-face building.

FLIRT was hers. Signed, sealed and delivered. The

best way to get over her embarrassment was to just embrace her temporary future.

The first step was to get out of the car.

Sydney opened the door to the Hyundai, planted both feet on the ground, stood and walked over. She prided herself that she looked over her shoulder only twice at the traffic sitting at the top of the hill at the red light.

The property was on a bit of a decline, so when she got to the front door, she couldn't see the drivers, and they couldn't see her.

Pacing the sidewalk, Sydney peered at the shop through critical eyes. Had the store been profitable in the past? How could she make it a success? What the hell was she doing?

Sydney pulled strands of hair from the corner of her mouth.

A war between confidence and failure tore her up inside. *I can't do this.* Then she imagined vacationing in Brazil and sighed.

That gave her seven hundred fifty thousand reasons to try.

Alone and slightly uncomfortable, Sydney wished she'd allowed Evette to be with her. She dialed and got her voice mail. "'Vette, give me a call. I signed the papers today. I'm outside the store wishing I had let you come with me. I know you offered." She laughed weakly. "You're a day older and smarter, I admit it. Give me a call later. Bye."

Another sigh left her.

It was just as well.

She needed to face her future before she could welcome anyone into it.

From the corner of her eye she spotted movement and held her phone tighter. Several men walked the pavement in front of the closed restaurant adjacent to her store and looked to be in an animated argument. They didn't look drunk. Just angry.

One consulted the others. Then all turned to stare at her.

The angriest man had angular lines to his face, as though he'd been pulled from the pages of a Ralph Lauren catalogue and dipped in impossibly smooth creamy cocoa.

He was tall and cut into a V that reminded her of a high school jock. And he wore black, from the tight T-shirt to the expensive pants.

When he lifted his arm and pointed at her, her taste buds burst.

He seemed to be calling her out, or beckoning her to him. She didn't know which, but she didn't intend to find out. Even from a distance she could see his furious eyes.

Lori's limousine pulled in, stopping the men from advancing toward her, and Sydney was glad for her extremely late arrival.

That didn't say much for chauffeur-driven limousines.

Sydney would put her faith in the Hyundai any day.

Lori climbed out halfway between the men and Sydney.

"Come this way, now." She immediately steered Sydney toward the door to the store, the key unlocking her future with a double click.

Suddenly Sydney wanted to take entering the establishment slower, but she didn't have time to choose. Lori ushered her inside with a hand at the center of Sydney's back.

Muggy, stale air greeted them as Sydney stood in the dark.

"I'll be right back," Lori said.

"Where are you going?"

"To get the lights."

She wanted to follow, but waited in dutiful silence, her nerves tight. When the lights flickered on, surprise crept over her like the human wave at a football game. FLIRT wasn't at all what she expected.

Then disappointment settled in.

The store had a convenience store feel, with pegged spinner displays and shelves stocked with stuff throughout the floor. There didn't appear to be any order, but moreso, it felt cheesy.

The fluorescent lighting didn't help by making everything look harsh and uninviting.

"This is it?"

"You can make it into what you want it to be."

Dust-covered surfaces and the clutter overwhelmed Sydney. This wasn't a place she'd want to visit alone. It wasn't sexy. "Was she profitable?"

Lori's mouth moved into a sympathetic curve. "Not as much as she wanted."

"Then why give it to me?"

"You're young. Your mother wanted you to have it all. You can do this, Sydney. We believe you can."

Tentatively she moved right, staring openly at penises in every color and size imaginable. Size ten? What kind of man was that big? And what woman would want a neon orange penis inside of her?

"There are women who find it extremely pleasurable," Lori said as if reading her mind. "Don't judge a dildo by its . . . packaging."

"This is unreal."

Lori slung her Chanel bag over her shoulder. "This is just the tip of the iceberg."

"What's that supposed to mean?" Sydney asked.

"That means if you're going to sell sex toys and earn your inheritance, you have to be friendly to your customers—and be able to help meet their needs. Women who purchase sex aids don't want to be judged. In the folder are the instructions on how to open, close, et cetera. The lights to the store are behind the storeroom door. I'm leaving now. If you need anything, call me, especially if anything gets crazy."

Sydney stopped her perusal and took the extended card. "Crazy like what?"

Lori gave her a wry smile. "You'll know when it happens. I'll see you at the opening."

Right, she reminded herself, she had three weeks before February fourteenth. "Wait." Sydney struggled to find more adequate words, but couldn't drag them into a coherent sentence. She was grateful for the opportunity, yet intimidated, and still didn't understand why her mother would do something like this.

Lori's dark green eyes stared inquisitively back at her as she waited in silence.

Sydney nodded. "Thank you."

"Good luck." Lori gave her a mock salute and

opened the door. A melody Sydney hadn't heard when they'd first entered tinkled the air.

Left alone for the first time, she huffed out a breath of anxiety and executed a slow turn, taking in every inch of floor space.

Maybe she could adjust the lighting. Then things wouldn't seem so harsh. Maybe add some mood music.

That was fine once the customers got in the store, but how would she get them there?

As Sydney contemplated, she moved to the left spinner and picked up an oval gadget with a handheld remote. She blinked rapidly when she realized it was a vibrating bullet. "Well, hell."

She balanced it in the palm of her hand, reading that it only required two AA batteries and a receptive woman. The door chimed, and the pointing man from down the walkway entered as if he owned the place. He walked straight for her, even as she backed up.

Sydney tried to hide the clitoral stimulator, but fumbled it into a somersault.

He snapped the mini vibrator out of the air. "I see you've made yourself right at home."

"It's my store," she said, immediately disappointed. Her voice lacked the confidence she needed to show him that she was in control. "And who are you?"

"Drew Crawford, owner of Satisfaction, the restaurant on the corner. I didn't expect this store to reopen. What's your name?"

"Sydney Morris."

"I heard that the owner passed away."

"She did."

He watched her closely as she headed toward the

center of the store. Sydney wouldn't go to the back in case she had to make an escape. Crawford didn't seem to want to hurt her physically, but there was a danger about him that made her edgy.

An undercurrent of anger coursed through him. She almost asked him to leave, but he wanted something. And she was curious.

"Was the owner someone close to you?" he asked.

"No, as a matter of fact, she wasn't."

"So why are you here?"

"FLIRT is my store."

He moved closer.

She gripped her hands together behind her back.

"How old are you?" he asked in a voice so low, her stomach jumped.

She tabled her desire to analyze the reaction and focused on Crawford's unwelcome presence during her first private moments in FLIRT. "None of your business. What do you want?"

"I'll get to that." He took his time looking her up and down. Sydney felt like a mannequin being stripped of her clothing at an all-male car show.

The prickly flush of desire drifted over her in a wave so thick she felt moisture gather between her legs. Not in recent memory had she reacted so strongly to a man. Drew Crawford was personally affecting her in a way she experienced only when she was home, in her bed alone.

She tried to sidestep him when her back met a huge display. Prepackaged penises in neon colors were pegged down her right side. Sydney didn't want to know what was sticking her in the ass. Suddenly the store, its contents, and this man were too much.

She looked at him, too stunned to move.

"That's what I'm talking about," he said as his dark gray eyes assessed her. "You're young, I'd say about twenty-four."

"I'm thirty-one."

"A thirty-one-year-old bookkeeper who doesn't have the experience to know how to use these toys, much less sell them. You're a fish out of water. Doing this out of an act of rebellion."

How could he know? "You don't know what you're talking about."

"Don't I? This suit is from the matron section of a department store, and you're wearing last year's black inch-and-a-half-soled shoes and grocery store stockings. Little gold studs in your ears, no mascara and not even a hint of lipstick. You work inside a building for ten hours a day, and you have a simple life. You don't sell dildos."

Moisture gathered in her eyes. She'd never had someone read her so accurately before. She'd been told she was suppressed, dull and even angry. But no one had ever guessed she was a bookkeeper. That offended her more than she cared to admit. If Drew Crawford stayed in her store, what else would he tell her about herself?

"Tell me I'm wrong," he said.

Sydney's legs began to itch. "You're wrong. You don't know anything about me."

"Did I insult you by saying you were a bookkeeper? I'm sorry." He touched his perfect abs in apology. "What do you do for a living?"

She swallowed the bitter taste of embarrassment. "I *was* a bookkeeper, but now I'm the sole prop-proprietor of this business." She forced herself to briefly meet his gaze.

He looked focused in the way she'd been long ago in college. Lately she'd settled into a vat of complacency that required minimal output. Each day she woke up, dressed, worked and repeated the same activity three hundred sixty-five times a year.

"Are you proud of what you do?" he asked.

Sydney mentally stepped away from the hot button. Reckoning was near, but he didn't need to know that. "Mr. Crawford, I'm a busy woman."

He pursed his mouth. "Fair enough. I'll buy this place for fifty thousand dollars. Cash."

He was so sure of himself, the smug SOB. Offering her unemployment so he could succeed. How dare he?

Even if she wanted to accept the money, she couldn't. She'd signed an ironclad contract with a dead woman's attorney.

"Are you afraid of a little competition?" she challenged. His eyes widened in surprise, and she could tell he didn't enjoy the shift in her approach to him.

"What we do is vastly different."

"Then you shouldn't mind my presence here. Different businesses, different income streams, different customers, but then again, maybe not. I trust you can find your way out."

Sydney had moved away from the spinner toward the door.

Drew didn't follow, but stuck out his finger and spun the rack. A ten-inch black dildo fell to the floor. He picked it up and started toward her.

He didn't hold it by the packaging, but by the base.

Sydney couldn't tear her gaze away from his hand around the powerful penis.

She'd backed into shelving that housed How-To DVDs, and one toppled to the floor. When he picked up the container, she read the title and felt as if she'd been set on fire.

How To Make Love To a Man.

Drew Crawford stood so close she smelled the spices on his clothing. He held the penis close to her. "Take it."

"Put it down."

"You know what to do with it, don't you?"

He was no longer challenging her aptitude as a businesswoman; he was testing her womanhood. She considered throwing it on the floor and jumping up and down on it, but changed her mind. He'd really think she was nuts.

Instead, she engaged in the pseudo tug-of-war and finally wrested it from his hand. She gazed at it lovingly and then smiled. "This is a toy. I like mine real and . . . bigger."

She thought she'd shock him, but the expression on his face was pure disbelief. "Sydney, you'll find that I'm a man who gets what he wants. My offer stands for twenty-four hours."

"No."

"Talk it over with your significant other. I'll check back in a day or two."

"It's my store. I make all the decisions, and my decision is to open in three weeks. Is there anything else—"

"Whoa. Three weeks from when?"

"Monday. I open February fourteenth."

"That's the day of *my* opening."

"Well, good luck. Is there anything else I can do for you?"

"Leave."

"That's not going to happen. Goodbye, Mr. Crawford."

"This isn't over," he assured her and walked to the door. "This is war."

5

Dread swept through Drew like fire to kindle as Mike waited outside of Satisfaction. He'd convinced his cousin to invest in his restaurant, and now they could lose everything because of the stubborn young woman inside FLIRT.

She was clueless. He could tell by the stunned look on her face when her vibrating bullet had flown into the air.

"What's the deal?"

Drew unlocked the door and inhaled the warmth as he walked inside. "The owner is deceased."

"So how'd this woman come into possession of the store?"

"I don't know. But she's got it. The funny thing is she's embarrassed by it. By the things inside. I saw her face. She doesn't know what she's doing."

"She's got to know something. I saw Lori King. She's

39

one of the sharpest estate attorneys in the country. If Lori represents her, the woman's legitimate."

Sydney Morris's sudden and unexpected appearance shocked him. Not like his family's party last night. Real shock.

Drew moved around the kitchen, tension coursing through his arms.

"But if it makes you feel better," Mike sighed, "I'll have King checked out anyway."

"Thanks." Drew opened the stainless steel refrigerator and brought out all of the fresh food he needed for a four-course breakfast. Donning his cap and coat, he methodically began to separate the items, then cook as he thought aloud his plan.

"Sydney Morris is young. I thought she might be in her twenties, but she said thirty-one. A bookkeeper who's as green as June grass. Five-six, one hundred twenty pounds, shoulder-length brown hair that has natural highlights when the light hits it right. Golden brown eyes, one-stud ear piercing. Freckle beside her right nostril, another one beside her left ear. Unmarried, unattached. Lives alone. No pets. Works out. Strong upper body."

"And her teeth?" Mike asked with a hint of facetiousness Drew didn't find amusing.

He washed his hands. "Corrected. White. Size seven shoe," he added, knowing his cousin's next question before he could ask it.

"Using your government training for the greater good, I see?"

Drew stirred the bubbling pots, rinsed the vegetables and started dicing them. "What else can I do with it? I'm retired."

"You didn't have to. You could have gone into the classroom and become an instructor. Even opened your own security agency."

"Every ex-agent wants to become his own boss. The thing is, you can't compete with the government. You can't just open your own agency and think you won't get your hands slapped. It's against the contract we all sign when we take the job. Besides, I've lived under the façade of being the dimwitted nobody everybody takes for granted for so long, I wouldn't know how to instruct a class. My entire adult life was built on a lie so that I could do my job of providing protection to my unsuspecting clients."

"Hell, I sure was surprised when I found out why you suddenly turned up on my doorstep last year." Mike looked up from the complicated coffee machine he was trying to turn on. "I may be a silent partner, but I insist upon a coffee machine a two-year-old can operate. This thing is ridiculous."

Drew wiped his hands, came over and pushed the On button, then went back to zesting lemon. "Lawyers," he sighed and shook his head.

Mike gazed at the dark liquid that spilled into the glass pitcher. "It's about damned time. Anyway, what was the name of the former owner?"

"Merry—like Christmas—Morris."

"And the woman who owns it now?"

"Sydney Morris."

"Sisters?" Mike asked as he stole a handful of blueberries from a bowl Drew had set on the table. He popped them into his mouth like peanuts.

"Does it matter?"

"Not really. Besides, we can do a property search, find out about the title that until last week was in the name of the deceased, then decide a course of action."

"I don't care what her connection to the deceased is. I don't want a porn shop opening down the plaza from my exclusive, expensive restaurant. I bought this place because they said that store would never open again. God rest the woman's soul, but her shop was supposed to go with her."

Drew set the first course before Mike, and he began to eat, the look of pure pleasure on his face giving the chef a modicum of comfort.

"Let's play what's the worst that can happen." Mike ate the fresh fruit, sprayed with lemon zest and sugar, and smiled.

"I take shipment on food, supplies, hire staff, pay insurance, and go into sky-high debt, then lose everything because the shop on the corner sells plastic dicks. The store wasn't even nice."

"According to whose standards?"

"Any decent person who visits that kind of establishment."

"No, really. What did it look like?"

"Seedy. Cheap. Not like I thought it would."

The look of enjoyment on Mike's face reinforced Drew's anger.

His restaurant deserved to come to life. And he wasn't going to let some bookkeeper who didn't know a vibrating bullet from a real one keep him from his dream.

Mike regarded him with the same serious eyes Drew had been facing all his life. All the Crawford men had gray eyes that could bore a hole into a man. Although in Drew's family, their eyes were more toward the darker end of the spectrum. Still, Drew felt the intensity facing his cousin.

"What is your ultimate goal?" Mike asked.

"Stop her from opening."

From across the restaurant Drew saw a car drive past the front window and head down the plaza.

They both watched as the car tore out of the driveway and careened into the street.

He'd been dicing tomatoes and put everything in a bowl and started for the door with Mike right behind. They'd gotten halfway up the sidewalk when the wind picked up white fliers and tossed them into the air.

Drew went for one stack while Mike went for another. GET OUT OR ELSE was spelled out in black block letters across the white paper.

The door to FLIRT burst open.

Sydney Morris came outside, the wind whipping her hair into stormy golden eyes. She ran around trying to catch fliers, then gave up when her arms were full. "Look what you've done. Are you crazy?"

"Who me?"

"You big buffoon," she screeched.

Drew looked at the irate woman, then at the flier in his hands. "I wouldn't waste my time. I already told you to leave."

"I'm calling the police. I won't tolerate this harassment."

She had determined little eyes, and he suddenly wondered if she was passionate in other areas of her life. "You'll know if I'm harassing you," he stated, matter-of-factly.

43

Her eyes narrowed as she searched for the hidden meaning.

"We came down here to see what was going on. Obviously I'm not the only one who doesn't want you here."

"That's too bad, Mr. Crawford, because I'm staying."

"We'll see about that."

The white-and-black fliers coated the winter grass, making the place look trashy. She was already bringing the wrong type of attention to this location. How would the governor feel about dining within a few yards of a sex-toy shop?

Sydney slammed the door to her store, but not before giving him a scathing look.

Mike had a stupid grin on his face as they went back to Satisfaction.

"What the hell is so funny?"

"Your life will get more interesting by the day."

"What do you mean by that?" Drew slammed the door on the cold winter air.

"I think you just met your wife."

Drew threw the fliers at Mike, who wasn't expecting a face full of paper. He laughed as he gathered up the sheets and stacked them neatly on a table. "What's wrong with you?"

"She's going to sink us with her anatomically correct plastic floats and nipple rings. This isn't funny." Drew washed his hands and went back to cooking. "What would I do with a mousy, skinny, angry woman anyway?"

Mike grinned, eating the delectable omelet Drew set before him. "I didn't know what I'd do with timid little Terra when I first met her. But I'll be damned if I didn't find out. To this day I won't let her wear pajamas in the bedroom. Man," he exclaimed. "Just thinkin' about her gives me the biggest—"

"Don't," Drew threw up his hand, not wanting to go there.

Terra was beautiful, as were all the Crawford wives. His cousins had been lucky to meet and marry the sexiest women alive. That fact wasn't lost on one of the few remaining single men in the family. But Drew couldn't imagine Terra in anything but a turtleneck and corduroy pants. Otherwise, Mike would know he'd once had the hots for his woman.

"I like my women bold and independent," he informed his cousin. "They know what they want, and they know where to get it. They flaunt their sexuality like a detective with a gold shield, and they want men like me because we don't get attached to anyone or anything. I'm a maintenance man, and the women I deal with only need touch-ups. Boring bookkeepers do nothing for me." Drew shivered at the thought of Sydney's frail body on his bed. "She's crazy, in case you hadn't noticed. How should we handle this?"

Mike shrugged. "Let's call the police and make a statement. Then we'll find out who Sydney Morris really is. Then we sue to stop her from opening."

Drew picked up Mike's plate and shoved the food down the garbage disposal.

"Are you crazy, messing with my food before I'm finished?"

"What the hell are you sitting there for? Get the papers drawn up. I want her served tomorrow and out of business by the weekend."

6

Sydney pulled on her four-year-old winter coat and shivered as she stepped into the biting January cold. She refused to wait inside because she didn't want the police in her store. She didn't want to endure their curious looks, or the judgmental stance they would probably take. Overcoming her own prejudice was enough for one day.

An hour had passed since she'd made the call, and the threatening fliers had blown across the parking lot and into the evergreen bushes. The place looked cheap and crummy. She grabbed a garbage can and started on one section of the property, yanking up fliers while clutching her coat.

It didn't take long to feel the air stream all the way to her bones as she leaned into a hearty wind that shook the phone lines overhead. Turning her back, Sydney let the freezing air swirl around her as she blew on her fingers to warm them.

Crawford was involved all right. She was fortunate to have seen him and his trusty sidekick. She just wished she'd caught them red-handed.

She'd have to mention to the police that he'd offered her a bribe right before he graduated into Intimidation 202.

Well, if that's how he wanted to be, fine. They didn't have to be friends.

Sydney huddled in her coat, her face in the collar, and looked back over the ground she'd covered. More fliers had blown into the area she'd just cleaned.

What a jerk. He'd wasted a perfectly good tree.

Dragging the can to the back of the store, she grabbed another and strengthened her resolve. He was going to have to do better than this to get her to close down. In fact, nothing he did would intimidate her.

She went for the more dense areas, but straightened at the sight of the patrol car.

A female officer sat behind the wheel, talking into a radio. She gave Sydney a measured look, and Sydney wasn't sure what was worse, being judged by a woman cop or a man.

Standing her ground, Sydney waited until the cruiser window was lowered.

"I'm Sydney Morris. I called you."

"Step back, please, ma'am."

Caught off guard, Sydney leapt back, and the officer got out of the vehicle. "I'm Officer Hutchins. What's the problem?"

"These." Sydney handed her the flier, her hand shaking from the cold. "I came outside, and they were strewn everywhere."

The officer's face was the perfect advertisement for the benefits of Botox injections. Her features never moved. "Are you the owner of FLIRT?"

"Yes, I am. Is that a problem?"

Officer Hutchins acted as if she hadn't heard Sydney's question. "What's your name again?"

"Sydney Morris," she said, growing defensive. "Look, I'm a tax-paying citizen who deserves to pursue my legitimate business without interference from anyone."

"I agree. But if you don't calm down, we're never going to get to the bottom of what happened here." She looked into the can. "Are these the same fliers?"

She made a sweeping gesture. "Yes. They're everywhere." Sydney's defensiveness slipped. "So you don't have a problem with what I do?"

The officer took off her mirrored glasses. She was a nice-looking woman with a silver wedding band on her third finger. She probably thought women who used sex toys for pleasure were desperate.

"I'm a woman *and* an officer of the law," Hutchins clarified. "I personally don't have a problem with your store. Professionally, you're a victim. It's my job to find the perpetrators, so why don't you tell me what happened."

An ally was more than Sydney expected. "I was inside the store, and when I came from the back, I heard voices. Two men from the restaurant next door were on my property with fliers in their hands."

The officer noted the location of the two businesses and wrote quickly on her handheld computer.

"Do you know the men?"

"One. His name is Drew Crawford. The other I didn't know, but they looked like brothers."

The officer's brows furrowed, but she didn't comment. Sydney wondered why this would cause a reaction, but didn't ask.

"When you caught them, were they disbursing the fliers?"

"Yes . . . well—"

Sydney closed her eyes and let the event replay in her mind.

Drew had been bent over. He'd reached for the fliers and stood up with them! Then she'd come outside.

She opened her eyes, confused. "I don't know."

"Tell me what you saw. Was he throwing them or not?"

"Not exactly. But he offered me fifty thousand dollars not to open my store."

"Why would he do that if he was going to throw fliers all over the place? And even on his property?"

"The offer was earlier today." Sydney put her cold hands to her eyes. "I believe he hired someone to try to intimidate me."

"Or maybe he wasn't involved at all."

"I don't think it's a coincidence that in the first few hours of taking possession of the store, I'm being threatened and harassed. This business has been known to attract unwanted attention."

Sydney stopped talking as another cruiser pulled down the lot, followed by an unmarked police car. Three men alighted from the green vehicle and walked toward the restaurant, oblivious to the cold and to her. The uniformed officer headed their way.

Sydney tried to stamp life into her numb feet as well as curb her sensitive temper, but the conversation wasn't going well. If Drew had been picking up the fliers, her comments to Hutchins wouldn't make sense. He'd said he wanted her gone. But littering? It was almost too immature for the bold man with a keen ability to read her.

"What's going on?" Hutchins asked the officer.

"Responding to a call from the owner of the restaurant. The detectives are friends of his. What have we got here?"

"Litter," Hutchins replied. "Ms. Morris, there's not a whole lot we can do. I'll write up a report, and you can call this number and get a copy."

"What about questioning him? I want you to ask him what he was doing here, and see if he'll confess."

"Hutch." The uniformed officer had already backed away as if to say 'no blood, no guts, no crime.' "Come here."

Hutchins went over, then walked back to Sydney, while he headed to the restaurant.

"I'll question the owner, and if anything turns up, I'll contact you. Otherwise, you can call in forty-eight hours for a report."

"What did he say?" Sydney stuck her chin out and tried to rally Officer Hutchins back to her side. "This isn't fair. I have a lot of work to do inside, but now I have to stand out in the freezing cold to pick up garbage thrown by my neighbor. Does that officer know anything?"

"He knows the owner of Satisfaction, and this type of activity isn't his style. I'll interview him, Ms. Morris, and if I find anything, the appropriate action will be taken.

Why don't you go back inside and warm up? I'll try to stop by before I leave."

The hopeful feelings from moments ago dissipated. "Don't let him off the hook because he's good looking. I hate to see people get away with murder because they show some teeth and touch their abs," she said, remembering.

Hutchins smiled. "Yeah, I hate that, too."

Sydney fought the wind and went back inside FLIRT, unsure if the officer was patronizing her.

Her face smarted, and her coat was ineffective. She stripped it off and wanted to toss it into the can with the offensive fliers, but didn't. She didn't have anything else to wear.

Angrily she paced the floor, hating that suddenly her life didn't seem to be offering her many choices.

What was the worst thing that could happen if she threw her coat away? She'd be cold until she bought another one. Her father would ask why she'd bought another when her current coat was still usable. Then she'd have to explain why she went against his wishes and took over FLIRT.

Staring at the garment that she'd dragged across the floor in her indecision, Sydney walked over to the trash can full of fliers and stuffed the coat in.

Elation swept through her, and she reveled in the emotion she'd let herself feel only a handful of times.

She sold sex toys! She'd thrown away her coat. And a confrontation with her father loomed on the horizon.

Chills raced over her arms, and Sydney craved heat. She still didn't know where the thermostat was.

Frustration pricked her bubble of self-empowerment, and doubt seeped out.

FLIRT was her store, and she had to get to know it over the next twenty-one days because once she opened, she had to be a selling machine to meet her quota.

Looking around, she shook her head. She had never been into marketing, but there were things that had to change. She grabbed fliers from the garbage can and started making notes on the back.

The lighting was all wrong. The spinners looked cheap. There probably wasn't anything she could do with the multicolored carpet, but she could soften it a bit. Lori had said the store had been moderately successful, but maybe with a few modifications, it could be so much more. Sydney walked the floor making notes and small diagrams. She backtracked, touching her forehead, confused.

She needed help. The store didn't feel right. It needed to be dolled up, and she knew just the person.

Sydney dialed Evette again.

"Hello?"

"Evette? Sydney. I got the store."

"Whooo—hoo!" Evette cheered as if she were at Turner Field. "Girl, what did your father say?"

"I haven't told him yet. I just signed the papers a few hours ago. Where were you? I could have used some moral support."

"Busy being stepmom to the men from hell."

Sydney sat on the stool behind the register and prepared for what would probably be a long conversation. For a woman who hated her job, Evette was the boss everyone wanted to have. She was the PR guru who made the debacles of celebrities seem like good deeds.

"I thought you were going to cut back on your hours?" Sydney said.

"I am. That's why I picked up my phone. Anyway, you need me to come over and buy something? My get-a-good-man habits are terrible, and I need a little satisfaction of the battery-operated variety."

"Ugh, don't utter that word to me again."

"What, variety?"

"No, satisfaction. That's the name of the restaurant next door. I met the owner, and let's just say he wants me gone. He offered me fifty thousand dollars to disappear."

"Take it!"

"I can't." Her heart palpitated that she had to turn down fifty grand. "I know it sounds wonderful, but I can't do it."

"Why?"

"I can't say."

"You can't what?" Evette was the master at keeping secrets, but that didn't stop her from trying to guess Sydney's. "If you can't say, then it must be something in the contract you signed today. Fine. You just better be getting way more money. So how does the store look?"

Sydney was relieved at the change in conversation. She didn't know how Lori King would find out if she told someone the terms of the agreement, but she believed the woman would know. And Sydney wouldn't jeopardize the ultimate payday.

"It's okay, but it needs work. I need your help, Evette. I'm not the marketing type, but I think I could make some updates, and the store would be more appealing. You have a good eye. I need some expertise."

"Sorry, doll. I know I just offered to come over and buy a huge dildo, but I'm swamped."

"Evette!"

"What should I say? Cock?" she asked innocently.

"You have such a filthy mouth."

Evette laughed in her throat, enjoying Sydney's embarrassment. "My mind is dirtier. Besides, you sell objects for sexual pleasure. What would you call a fake penis? And please don't go suburban on me and give it a stupid name like manhood, or joystick. They sound so asinine."

Sydney giggled nervously. Evette had her beat, and she knew it. "I just can't fix my mouth to say dick or cock or prick or any of the other words I've heard to explain a man's anatomy. They all sound nasty and slightly hookerish."

"That's a new word," Evette said, laughing.

"I made it up."

"So how would you describe it? Tell me and then I have to go."

Sydney straightened her spine, smiling. "I'd say it was his . . . business."

Evette gurgled. A lot. Then coughed. "His *business?* I think that might be a record-setting entry in the category of ridiculous."

"Evette! That's not fair. I think it is his business."

"Syd, it's corny. Use it in a sentence."

"No, I'm not playing phone sex with you."

Evette laughed. "Uh, honey, I prefer my sex talk with a whole lot more bass and masterful delivery with his *business.* Come on, shy girl. Use business in a sentence or you have to use dildo or cock. Honestly, I don't think you can."

Sydney had accepted two challenges today and won. The store was hers, and she wasn't going to be pushed out by Crawford. Why not three for three?

"I like a man who will give me his business any time, any day, anywhere I choose."

"Surprisingly good, but more personal. Something about being naked and business."

Sydney walked to the back of the store, pulling the garbage can, the phone to her ear. Talking, she pushed open the back door leading outside.

"When I'm soaking wet after a bath, I want my man to dry me off and use his business to tease and satisfy me all night long."

Silence hung between the two friends; then Evette started clapping. "Hot damn, I think we've got a winner!"

Sydney burst out laughing, when the garbage can was gently pulled from her hand.

"What the—"

"I hate to interrupt what sounds like a very interesting conversation, but this is my garbage can."

Drew looked at Sydney with a mixture of curiosity and shock on his face. They both heard the loud squeal from the receiver, and Sydney knew Evette was probably having a nervous breakdown.

The phone slipped from Sydney's hand and toppled into the can with the big *S* on the side.

Why hadn't she seen that before?

"I didn't realize . . . here."

She released the can and wished she could shrink to the size of an ant and slip into the cracks on the floor. Even in the blistering cold, she could feel heat climbing up her back and neck, coming to rest in her cheeks. She crossed her arms over her chest because her breasts were her body's next emotional giveaway. Her nipples stuck out like high beams on an Escalade.

She had no recourse but to stand there and deal with him.

"Um, sorry," she said.

He ignored the apology and looked her in the eye. "You're at least an interesting bookkeeper."

Sydney held herself tighter. "I'm glad you're amused."

"No," he said, coming inside the back door. "Intrigued."

He touched her arm with his finger, and she dropped her arms. Her breasts bloomed like sunflowers in spring.

He clicked inside his jaw. "That's quite a greeting."

Sydney drew her arms back up and locked them in place. Embarrassment flared all over her body, and she wished she could go to another room and pull herself together. But Drew was inside her back door, and he wasn't leaving.

"I'm nervous. So please—"

"You shouldn't be. We're two adults."

"Leave," she said, wishing she could shove him outside. But if she moved her arms, her breasts might just walk over and plaster themselves on his face. She couldn't believe how strongly her body was reacting to him. She kept Band-Aids in her purse for this type of situation. She'd need at least twenty to mask this reaction.

"Don't you have guests?" she demanded. "Friends to powwow with on how you're going to get rid of the sex-shop girl next door?"

"Despite what you think, you aren't the topic of my

every conversation. I might want you gone, but I have other things going on in my life. So I'll just take my garbage can."

He bent down, and Sydney wanted to melt. He was inches from her distended left nipple.

"Just what do you think you're doing?" she asked, slightly hoarse.

A few seconds passed, and he stood up and handed her the phone from the garbage can. "This belongs to you." He pushed open the door and pulled his can outside. "Just so you know, I'm going to think about you after I go in that door to my apartment to take care of a little . . . business."

His look set her on fire. Sydney didn't miss the meaning, but with the strength of ten men didn't glance below his waist to see what effect she'd had on him. She was already embarrassed. Falling down wouldn't help.

She kept one arm in place over her chest and grabbed the door bar. "As you said, I'm sure you have other things to think about. You probably do need to rest after all the wasted energy you expended in your failed intimidation attempt."

A ghostly smile crossed his face as he leaned in. "One day I'm going to have my business so deep in you, you're going to cry out my name right before you fall apart in my arms."

Sydney's mouth fell open.

"You never have to guess what I'm thinking. Throwing fliers is child's play. Something I never indulge in. Your apartment upstairs is right next to mine. Stop over any time you want some . . . business."

Unsteady on her feet and unable to hold the door

open any longer, Sydney let it close. Not that it mattered. He'd already walked into a headwind as if he weren't affected by the cold.

She stood there, her nipples aching, her head light.

What was he talking about, her apartment? Rushing back into the store, Sydney grabbed the keys Lori had given her and ran out the front door.

7

"So where's the hottie that I heard on the phone yesterday?" Evette walked through the store for the fifth time. She'd drawn a sketch of the place and was now comparing her diagram to Sydney's.

"I don't know and I don't care."

Sydney caught a glimpse of the two diagrams as 'Vette passed. Her own was plainly sketched with a number two pencil on the back of the offensive flier. Crude lines made up the walls, and square boxes outlined the checkout counter. She'd taken only a few seconds and the side of the pencil to shade in the floor, while Evette's had been done with a ruler, colored pencils and attention to detail Sydney hadn't even considered.

Embarrassment knocked at the door of her conscience, but was denied access. She wasn't an interior decorator. Decorating a sex shop had never fallen into the realm of her real world. Crude, as far as she was concerned, was better than nothing.

"Where are you, Syd?" Evette swung her arms in the air, capturing her attention. "You haven't completed one task since we got here."

"Yes, I have." Sydney looked up at the unit she'd been merchandizing and sighed. Evette was right. Her plan had been to remove all the low-selling edible body gels and replace them with the hottest sellers, but she'd shelved them all. Again. "I thought doing it this way was best."

"Sure you did. Of course you want to keep the gels that you've only sold two of on top. That's a brilliant plan."

"Don't be a smart mouth."

Sydney didn't want to admit that her thoughts had been on the man who'd invaded her back hall yesterday. The whole thing about falling apart in his arms had stayed with her.

She didn't know who Drew thought he was, but she wasn't the type to have sex with men who crudely assumed she would give it up in a hallway.

Who was she kidding? She wasn't the type to have sex, period.

But damnit, the thought of sitting on top of him kept looping through her mind as if it were one of the lasso ropes that was hooked on the chain-link contraption in the corner.

"Focus," she murmured. Concentrating on a task had never been so difficult, but she felt challenged as her thoughts zinged from the store, to her mother, to Drew Crawford, then to her father.

Sydney finally closed her eyes. *One battle at a time.*

Opening them, she didn't allow herself to blink until she'd removed all the low-selling items and placed the top sellers eye level in neat rows. Victorious, she satisfied her need to blink and reached into the box and grabbed a couple of the cherry-flavored gels. Checking to make sure Evette wasn't looking, she squirted a bit on her hand and sampled it. The taste wasn't bad, but would *he* like it?

Frustrated, Sydney began to hum low in her chest in one long stream that wasn't musical. No one could hear the soundless exhalation unless she got louder. And she rarely did.

Sydney recognized the defense mechanism for what it was. Her attempt to ward off the uncomfortable feelings that dealing with Drew Crawford elicited.

The way he'd breathed on her nipple made her want to knock him over the head. Or, she blinked rapidly, offer him a taste.

Sydney sighed, moving to the second shelf.

Fingering the other bottles, she couldn't fight the picture of him in her mind. He didn't seem like the type who'd like gels or anything else but him in the room with a woman.

He's an unfriendly man, she reminded herself. He didn't like her, and he wanted her to close down so she could fail and he would succeed. That was more than enough reason to hate him.

Contemplating his preference for gel or no gel wasn't in her best interest.

Everything about him said he was accustomed to getting his way. But not with her.

Sydney hurried through the rest of her shelving, determined not to think of him intimately.

She was going to succeed. Even if he got angry.

Even if her father got angry.

"Is there music in this joint? It's sure quiet in here."

Thankfully Evette's interruption was well-timed. "I think there's a sound system in the back. I'll go check. I need to know anyway."

Evette was oblivious to her struggle, and for that Sydney was grateful. How awful would it be for her best friend to know that she was more comfortable in the store than Sydney was?

Would she laugh if she knew that owning FLIRT was Sydney's one and only attempt at striking out on adulthood without her father's approval? That she needed this to break the tie between them because she didn't know any other way?

Sydney shook her head as the truth radiated through her. She wanted the store.

Being in it for the past two days had shown her the potential. And she wanted a chance to be her own woman. With or without her father's approval.

In a way, the thought put her at ease.

The other side of her knew she'd have to deal with her dad soon enough.

From the boxes in the back, she gathered one sex toy from each, determined to get to know them . . . intimately. For good measure she threw in some gels and condoms. If she was going to sell these items, she was damn sure going to be an expert. She scrawled her name on the box and put it by the back door to take home later.

Standing several feet behind the stockroom door, the sound system was stacked with a CD player, receiver and a box Sydney couldn't identify. Cords ran down the back of the equipment, and she followed them to the outlet. They all seemed to be plugged in, but still no sound, no matter how often she pushed the On button.

Syd finally gave up. "Sorry, kiddo. I don't know how to get the thing going. If I try to figure it out, I might try to rewire the whole building."

"Please don't do that," Evette said. "I remember the last time you helped me with my system. I almost never figured out how to work it."

"You had a bad receiver."

"More like I had a bad installation tech. Maybe your Mr. Sexy Voice can help."

Evette squeezed by Sydney's shopping cart full of merchandise and headed for the section of dildos. She started pulling them off the spinner and putting them on the floor.

"I was thinking we'd line those up on one wall," Sydney said. "The hottest sellers in the center. The most expensive ones at eye level. What do you think?"

"Brilliant."

"Is that your new word?"

Evette looked at her and smiled. "Well, I'm kind of dating two guys. One is this British guy from work. Everything with him is smashing or brilliant. Sorry, I guess he's rubbed off on me."

"How long have you two been going out?" Syd asked, slightly hurt. She lived vicariously through Evette.

"We started about two weeks ago. Right about the time—"

"Merry died," Syd finished. "You could have still told me."

Evette shrugged, regarding her carefully. "You were busy with life. Besides, I hate to talk about a guy when nothing is going to come of it. As far as I'm concerned, men fall into two categories. Marriageable or maintenance."

Sydney glanced at Evette out of the corner of her eye. "You still don't want to get married."

"Correct."

"Is he married?"

"No, and he wants to keep it that way."

"Perfect for you." Evette hadn't wanted to get married ever since middle school when it seemed as if every family on their block got divorced, including Sydney's. Strangely enough, Evette's parents were still together. "What happens when one of you changes his mind?"

"We go our separate ways. Those are the rules. Why aren't you dating, Syd? I put money on you going buck wild once you moved out of your father's house, but that was three years ago and so far, nothin'."

Referencing her inventory sheet, Sydney tossed the low-selling novelty cards into the shopping cart. "I hope you didn't lose much. There just weren't a lot of guys running up to ask me out."

"You have to break your routine. Pulling a freestanding boxing bag out of your garage and onto the driveway so you can beat the shit out of it isn't a man's fantasy of a woman he wants to date."

"Tough. That's what I enjoy. And if the health club around here offered boxing, I'd join, but they don't. So it's not really my fault."

"Of course it's not." Evette shook her head, falsely agreeing with Sydney. "You're a thirty-one-year-old virgin who doesn't seem to care that she needs sex to complete her life."

Laughter burst from Syd's mouth. "First of all, I'm not a virgin."

"Technically you might be right, but, sweetie, be for real. One guy groped your breasts and came, and the other one came on your stomach. That hardly constitutes the complete act of making love."

Sydney sputtered while laughing. "Shut up! I told you he got it in before his untimely end. Besides do we have to relive all of my most embarrassing moments? That'll teach me to confide in you again."

"I'm merely using those examples to help you."

"Do what? Kill myself? Goodness!"

Evette ignored Sydney's chagrin as she had all their lives. Instead she placed the fake penises by size on the newly constructed wall pegs.

"What about the other guy?" Sydney asked.

"Mmm. He's delicious and sweet and a hunk. Every time I see him, I want to strip naked. My heart just flutters whenever I'm around him."

"So what's the deal?" Syd asked, helping Evette with the wall.

"He's got baggage and—" 'Vette stopped talking, her hands slowing.

Syd noticed it all, but said nothing. This guy was important. "And?"

"And he's not black."

"Okay."

'Vette looked at her for a moment, then kept working. "You're fine with that?"

" 'Vette, There are so many women looking for love. Why should I tell you what color it should come in?"

"I figured you'd say that. But there's more."

Sydney climbed the stepladder and accepted the vibrators from her friend. "What? The baggage and the fact that you don't like it?"

"That's right."

"Maybe he's worth it, I don't know. Keep me posted."

"I will," Evette said. "Anyway, back to you. If you want to get the hooker of the year award, you have to go all the way. With multiple people."

Sydney laughed. "Hooker of the year? We made that up when, high school?"

"Yep. So, what happened with Mr. Sexy Voice from yesterday? Did you go up to the apartment?"

"No. I went home."

"Gracious, how could you? He sounded sexy as hell. Plus, all that talk about his business? I got hot just listening to him."

Syd covered her ears, laughing hard. "You're a freak."

"True," Evette said and stopped. "Let's go up to the apartment."

"Why would I want to?"

"Because it's yours. Come on." Evette started for the back room.

"No! I mean, it was my—Merry's. Why would I want to go into her apartment?"

"Are you ever going to face your past? Because I'm getting damned tired of dancing around the land mines in your life."

"I don't want to go up there, Evette. Can't you understand that?"

"No, Syd. You own the store your mother left to you. It's not just because you want whatever that contract promised you. You want to know about her. You once loved her. I don't see the harm in visiting her apartment."

"Because she was there, 'Vette! This store was hers, but it wasn't personal. Her apartment is all about her. That's why I don't want to go. Do you get it now?"

Evette held a navy blue penis in her hand. "That's exactly the reason to go, but I respect your wishes. All I know is that if it were my mother and she thought enough to leave me a store that's worth probably about a million bucks, I'd want to know about her."

"Can we agree to disagree and let it go?"

Evette hurried over and hugged her. "Of course."

They both turned as a key turned the lock in the door.

A woman with purple hair and enough face piercings to set off the security equipment at the airport walked in cursing softly. "It's cold enough to freeze my tits off."

Sydney couldn't guess her age, but she wasn't super young. She was anywhere between forty and sixty.

She walked over to Sydney. "You favor Merry, so I guess you're the boss now. I'm Chyna with a *Y*. I go by Chyna. I work here. Worked for your mother," she said, fingering the cards in the basket. "Work for you now, if you're keeping me. Probably should tell me now before I take my coat off. You should know that I'm gay. But I don't hit on customers."

She pushed her locks off her neck and wiped her face with her glove. "I have lots of gay friends, and they support the business. So from time to time, they come in the store, and I talk to them. Your mother loved me and I loved her. She was a dear lady, even though she was straight. God rest her sweet soul, damnit, so do you have a problem with me being here and me being gay?"

"No." Sydney watched the ageless woman walk around the store assessing the changes that had been made. "You're doing a damned fine job."

"You have a key," Sydney stated.

"Yep and I use it to open the store and close occasionally. Got a problem with that?"

"No," Syd said.

Evette looked at Syd and shrugged as if to say *I don't know what to make of her either.*

Chyna walked over to Sydney. "Answer quickly. Do you have a problem with a gay woman working for you?"

"I said no, but I don't want you to think just because you're gay you can wear it like a badge of honor and get on your pedestal and lecture me or anyone else about it. I'm heterosexual, thank you very much, but that's the last time I'll bring it up. If we're going to work together, it's about mutual respect. And you have to come to work on time."

A slow smile spread across Chyna's face. "Good deal. You're not the least bit homophobic. That's damned good. We get all types in here. I can handle them, but as the owner you have to have an open mind." She walked over to Evette.

"Sweetie," Evette said. "I'm totally into men. But I'd

love to go dancing at the club with you sometime. I had a ball last month at Celebrity."

Chyna's smile deepened. "You got in? It was standing-room only. That O'Chello woman can sing her ass off."

Chyna slipped her coat off, looking around. "I really love what you've done. You've got a good eye."

"Thanks," Sydney said, feeling a sense of comfort come over her. "I want to do something with the lighting to soften the—"

"Rug," they said together and laughed.

"I told Merry it was the most garish thing she could have ever bought, but at the time she wasn't thinking long term," Chyna said. "Eventually I'd like to see it replaced with something black-and-white. Maybe a zebra print."

Sydney shared her notes with her employee. "I had that down. We're on the same track. Amazing."

Sydney hadn't realized she and Chyna had been chatting for a while until Evette walked up with her coat on. "You two look like a match made in sex-shop heaven, so I think I'm going to shove off and get to work."

"Come on, Evette. We have tons to do."

Evette smiled. "I'll be back later. I've got to get my new vibrator. As soon as you learn how to operate the register."

"Right." Syd bit her lip. "Maybe Chyna could show me."

"Ladies, have fun," Evette said, blowing her a kiss. "See you later."

"Okay."

Evette headed into the cold, slamming the door behind her.

"We could move this cage to the side," Chyna suggested, looking at the notes Sydney had written down. "And put the S&M videos beside it."

"Oh," Sydney said, feeling her face heat up. She hadn't known what the cage was for or the chains and lassos linked to it. "I've got a lot to learn."

A knock sounded on the locked door, and Sydney headed for it. "Evette must have forgotten her keys."

She opened the door and was startled to see two sheriff's deputies. "What can I do for you?"

"This is an order for you to cease and desist operation of this business immediately."

Shocked, Sydney looked at her hand. "What?"

"You're closed for business, starting now."

Sydney looked back at Chyna, who appeared royally pissed.

Sydney closed the door on the police and passed Chyna as she headed straight to the stockroom.

"You're on the clock," Sydney said over her shoulder. "Call my attorney, Lori King."

Chyna gave a little leap, grinning as she caught up to Syd. "You got it, boss. Uh, where you going?"

Sydney shoved her arms into her brand-new winter coat.

"There's a bully next door who's begging for round two."

8

The door to the restaurant burst open, and the silhouette of the pink-frocked intruder stopped as she stood wide-legged in the doorway.

Drew had his 9 mm pointed at her head before he could stop himself. He'd reacted instinctively to the threat, but luckily his brain was faster than his hand or he'd have shot Sydney on the spot.

He stood behind her, having just finished installing a bench that would hopefully keep those waiting comfortable. The muzzle of the automatic weapon was easily an inch from her scalp, but he drew it back.

"Where are you, you spineless jerk?" Sydney Morris yelled into his restaurant.

"I presume that would be me."

She spun around, clearly surprised. She jumped back a foot when she saw the gun.

He had holstered it, but she couldn't stop staring at it. "What can I do for you?"

"What is that—are you going to shoot—Ah!" she yelled, her fists clenched.

Furious, she stared at him. In his lifetime Drew had seen his share of tantrums, but never by a woman in a soft pink wool coat.

He grabbed the door, closed and locked it and went in the kitchen. "Coffee?"

She stormed in, and that's when he noticed the pink Burberry boots. *Wow. Cute.*

"I didn't come over here to play tea party with you. I want you to know you don't scare me. Except for the gun." She stared at his waist.

"Anything else?" he asked.

"I'm not leaving. I'm going to open for business, and you'd better get used to the idea, buddy. Getting your friends in high places to do you favors is only going to go so far. I have friends, too, you know."

Drew braced his hands on the stainless prep table and watched Sydney. She was mad. And although he'd had a gun pointed at her head mere seconds ago, she hadn't backed down. Either she was very stupid or very naive. Something in him wanted to know which.

"Does anyone know you're here?"

"What? Why?" She glanced at his waist and then up. "You're going to shoot me and do what? Bury me in the snow? For your information, the police are at my store."

"They left right after your friend in the powder blue Lexus convertible drove off. Black woman, approximately thirty-two or thirty-three, six feet, one hundred sixty pounds, brown hair, brown eyes, right-handed and talks. A lot. Winter must be hell on her car."

"Who are you, Adrian Monk? And who cares about her car?" Sydney demanded. "The sheriff's deputies can come right back if you try anything. My employees know I'm here."

"That would be one employee, a strange lady with purple locks. Black woman, five-four, noticeable limp from scoliosis or an injury, indeterminate age. Gay."

"Do you get your kicks watching me, my friends and my staff? What kind of freakish chef are you?"

Drew wanted to laugh, but instead poured two steaming cups of coffee. He added his special blend of cream and sat down in the nearest booth. "Care to join me?"

Sydney stomped over to him, the cease and desist order in her hand. "How can you sit here drinking coffee when you know you're wrong for trying to close me down?"

"It's nothing personal, but you aren't supposed to be there."

"Who said, you? You don't rule the world."

"I bought this restaurant because I was assured that your store would never open, no disrespect intended to the deceased. Sit down. Let's talk about this like two reasonable people."

Sydney seemed to be sizing him up as she considered what to do. She finally scooted on the bench, eyeing him warily. Her fingers slid around the fine bone china he'd picked out himself in the native country, and he hoped her fit didn't include breaking things.

"It's very good," he assured her.

"I don't want your coffee. I want to call a truce."

Drew wrapped his hands around the cup, when he really wanted to wrap his hands around her. "You're propositioning me?"

"Yes, if that's what you want to call it. Why don't we agree to not operate on the same days? That way your customers won't be tempted to spend their dinner money in my store."

Before he could help himself, Drew burst out laughing. "I'm sorry, I can see you're serious."

She rolled her eyes, showing how he'd stretched her patience. "I could open Thursday through Sunday—"

"That's peak time for me. People eat on the weekend in case you didn't know. Why don't you open Sunday through Thursday and close on the weekend?"

"That won't do because people buy movies and—and *things* for their weekend pleasure."

"What things?" he asked easily.

She lifted her cup to her lips and drank. Her eyes never wavered, and he had to give her points for staying cool. But the rising color in her cheeks gave her away.

He thought of her other reaction the last time they'd met and wondered what her breasts were doing now.

"Never mind what things!" she said hotly. "I came over here in good faith to offer a compromise, when I didn't have to. But I can see you want to fight dirty."

"Is there any other kind?"

Drew watched the woman with the honest face, and he sipped his coffee to give himself something to do besides touch her. He hadn't been prepared for the shop to reopen. But now that Sydney was doing just that, he had to protect his investment.

They sat in silence, and she finished her coffee.

"Make me a counteroffer," she said, eyeing him. "I don't want to fight with you."

"My offer still stands."

"What off—" she said, then set her cup down. "I'm not for sale. *FLIRT*," she stressed, "isn't for sale."

She got up and repositioned her coat until she felt comfortable. "I can see we aren't going to agree on anything. It's a shame you don't see the value in compromising."

"Merry Morris was the mother you were estranged from since you were a little girl. Why do this to yourself?"

"How do you know that?" The anguished whisper tore at his decision to stop FLIRT from existing. It also made his heart ache. Drew had begun to feel this way nearly two years ago and attributed his getting shot to those "feelings."

He'd trusted the wrong person. And now he was going to have to make up for the wrongs of the past.

"I know about you because people tell me things, Sydney. From my own observations, you don't fit in that type of store."

She glared at him. "What do you know about me?"

"I know you're a thirty-one-year-old bookkeeper who is an only child to the man who raised her. Your mother left when you were in grammar school, and you've had very little contact with her since. You lived a good life."

"What would you know about that?"

"Every other person comes from a broken home. That's reality. Your life probably wasn't perfect, but whose is? Merry willed you her store, and from my personal observations, I would guess you don't know how to use one thing in there. With all the baggage from your past, why would you want to own it?"

She purposely moved her cup away from the edge of the table to the center and stepped back. "You found out a few tidbits about me and my mother and you think you can typecast me into the life you think I had?"

"I can't typecast what's true, Sydney. How long can you stay in a business you don't know how to run?"

"I have a degree in business, mister. Besides, what I know is none of your business. Your legal maneuvering isn't going to deter me."

"You've got enough money to fight the city?"

Her eyes accused him of awful things. Despite the fact that he knew he was fighting for a good reason, her pain stung him as if a swarm of bees had made him their target.

"I guess you'll have to find out."

An empty threat, he thought. Made by a desperate woman.

"Last chance. Fifty thousand dollars. Guaranteed. Take it and make a life for yourself. No strings attached. Any agreements you made can be broken. I can take care of it."

Fear filled her eyes, and he knew he'd gone too far.

Drew cursed under his breath as she backed away, looking at him as though he was alien.

"I don't know who you think you are, but if you come near me or my store again, I'll have you arrested."

9

I'll take care of it.

The words beat on Sydney's neck and back where tension owned the most real estate.

Her father had used those same words twenty-one years ago. The day her mother had left.

Nausea rocked her stomach, so she closed her eyes, held her breath and wished the world still. Sydney felt as sick now as she had then.

Why were men always offering to take care of something for her? Did they think she was weak and incapable?

Obviously. She wasn't treated like a female tycoon, but rather an incompetent mailroom clerk.

Like Lenny Morris's offer years ago, Drew was attempting to persuade her to buy into something she wasn't going to like. Something that wasn't in her best interest.

But he'd get exactly what he wanted.

How convenient.

Stopping abruptly at the red light, Sydney clutched the steering wheel of the Hyundai and wished the streaming January rain would take up residence in another state.

Right now she needed sunshine. She needed to be outside, her sneakers hitting the asphalt as she circled beautiful Piedmont Park. She craved the excited sound of dogs barking while helmeted rollerbladers whizzed by, so she could take all those noises and cast them away and get lost in her own thoughts. She did some of her best thinking at the park.

A blaring horn and flickering bright lights from the SUV behind her motivated Sydney to join the present world.

She stomped on the accelerator too hard and jerked forward, before turning down one street, then up another. The announcer on the radio annoyed her just before she cut him off.

Despite the groundhog's prediction of an early spring, there would be six more weeks of winter. A storm was brewing over Texas and was supposed to hit Georgia in four days.

Sydney drove, cognizant only of the fact that she wasn't heading toward home. She couldn't go to the empty house and do nothing all evening.

Drew Crawford had pissed her off with his I-spy abilities and the confident way he'd offered to buy off her life.

She'd been unnerved by him, but angry for reasons he'd never believe. She didn't know anything about running a business, and she didn't know anything about her product. That much was true.

The burning question on her mind since she'd left his restaurant was *how* would she become a success?

Turning right onto Peachtree Street, she saw the bookstore and made her way into the left turn lane. The only way to know anything was to get educated. Sydney parked and ran into the two-story bookstore.

"May I help you?" The bored, expressionless clerk had his head down and looked at her over the frames of his plastic glasses.

"I'm looking for books on running your own business."

"Up escalator. Right and right."

"Thanks." She started off, then doubled back. "Is there a restaurant around here?"

"Café upstairs. Right, straight."

A man of few words. She appreciated him after the day she'd had.

"Thanks again."

No response. Fine. Men were exhausting.

Four hours later, Sydney stretched her body and heard the embarrassing snaps it made from being curled up and hunched over too long.

She put her hands on her hips and leaned back and was rewarded with a few more pops. Gathering the books she'd been reading, she headed for the cart reserved for books that needed to be reshelved, separated out the ones she wanted to keep and was shocked at the amount she put back.

How did bookstores make money when people were

allowed to read to their hearts' content and then no
make a purchase?

No wonder so many stores were closing. The con
sumer was allowed to do things today that would hav
been frowned upon twenty years ago. People were doin;
a lot of things differently these days. Like willing se
shops to their daughters.

She stopped at the café counter.

"Order?"

The same young man who'd given her directions wa
now working in the café. "You've moved up," she saic
trying to strike up a conversation.

When her overture wasn't reciprocated, she gazed a
the menu. "Mango tea with a chocolate chip cookie."

"Three seventeen."

Sydney paid and fingered the books she'd chosen t
buy.

He gave her the tea, and she had to make two trip
before she had everything on a table.

Although she hated the word *dummy*, she had two c
their books and a whole host of others that talked abou
inventory, taxes, financing, payroll, hiring staff and s
much more.

All the books stressed that she must believe in herse.
and what she was doing in order to make it, but even
book pointed out that the failure rate of new businesse
was nearly three times the success rate.

She had only one advantage going for her.

The business had been successful before.

Sydney flipped to a blank page in the journal she'
bought for notes and started a list.

Call Lori King. Stop the injunction. Have Chyna fi

out tax papers. Complete store inventory. Get to know the products. She was scratching more items on her list when bells rang overhead.

"The store will be closing in ten minutes. Please take your purchases to the register now. Thank you for shopping at Great Bookstore."

The line formed slowly and snaked into the rows with the intellectual greats like Plato and Socrates, while Sydney hurried into the marketing section and grabbed two books. How could she have forgotten?

Advertising was essential. All the books said so, after being allowed to operate.

Weighted down, she got to the counter and slid four stacks of books on the countertop.

The couple behind her kissed and talked quietly, then turned the tide of their conversation to her books. "Opening your own business someday?"

Sydney nodded, but didn't elaborate.

"Any idea what it's going to be?"

The redheaded woman stepped to her side, and Sydney glimpsed the woman's T-shirt.

He died for you and me was emblazoned across her stomach with a bleeding hand above it.

Sydney avoided her eyes. "A general idea."

This wasn't a conversation she wanted to have while thirty people in line looked on.

"That's a lot of books to not know what you want to do." The woman smiled brightly in her assessment.

Was she being judgmental? Sydney cocked her head to the side. "I'm the owner of a sex shop. I sell dildos, delicious body gels, porno movies and water mats for men who want a little hanky panky while lounging in

their swimming pools. If you'd like to come by some
time, I'd love to see you. My store is named FLIRT, and
I'm open for business February fourteenth. All of you
drop by." She looked at the clerk. "Please put this on my
American Express."

She turned to the pale woman whose once smiling
mouth was now opened in a shocked *O*. She reminded
Sydney of the inflatable raft woman. "I need the fre-
quent flyer points."

Patrons in line started clapping as her four-hundred-
dollar purchase was paid for and bagged.

The clerk put his name on a store card and slipped it
into her bag. "You need a good salesman, call me."

"Hey." A woman called to her from the row of books
on sexuality. "If you don't already have lingerie, can you
carry some in plus sizes? I have a hard time finding sexy
items for bigger women."

Sydney smiled. "Consider it done."

The woman grinned, and she was big and beautiful.
"I've been in a few of those stores, but I'm put off by the
lack of help. Maybe you could have staff that talks to
people, explains things. Not everybody that shops in
those stores are perverts."

"I know," Sydney agreed. "Don't worry. A knowledge-
able staff will be on duty at all times."

"Then I'll see you there. Here." She gave Sydney two
books. "You're going to need these."

Sydney read the titles. *Seductive Letters*, volumes ten
and eleven. She put her heavy purchases on the floor
and glanced through the pages. They were letters from
people recounting hot sexual experiences.

She felt an internal tug, and her eyebrow shot up.

Why not? She had a full magazine section. She'd order one set and see how they sold.

"I hate to get back in that line."

The woman waved and got the cashier's attention.

"These two books, I'm paying for."

Sydney gave her a quick hug. "Thanks. Come in my store and I'll make sure you're taken care of."

"You got a card?" a couple asked as she walked toward the exit. "We'll support you."

Sydney fished out her brand-new journal book and tore a page off the rings. "I don't, but here's the address. Come by February fourteenth and I'll give you ten percent off your entire purchase."

The offer was made to everyone who stopped her, and at a quarter after ten, fifteen minutes after the store officially closed, Sydney got into her car.

A fit of laughter shook her as she cheered for herself.

Not only had she bought books on how to run a business, but the people in line weren't prudish or judgmental. It seemed they were more like her than not.

Energized, she pulled out her to-do list and dialed Lori King's number.

"King."

"Where've you been?"

"Who is this?"

"It's Sydney Morris. I apologize for calling so late, but we have a situation with Drew Crawford."

"I see. And to answer your first question, I was at a funeral and took some personal time."

"I'm sorry." Stunned into silence, Sydney felt herself wanting to have respect for the dead person, and for the weariness and pain in Lori's voice. "I can call you in a few days."

"I'll be fine. Your situation can't wait. Look, I was your mother's attorney. If you'd like me to be yours, you'll have to pay me."

"Funny, you didn't mention that before."

"It's been a long day. I'm sad and I'm tired. My retainer is ten thousand dollars. Crawford is a powerful name in this state, and to some, they can do no wrong. If you want the best, you'll have to pay for it."

"Ten grand is a lot of money." Sydney thought of her bank account and how thin it would be if she paid the retainer. But she'd committed to this dream; it was hers to achieve or lose.

"I don't make promises I can't keep, so don't get it in your head I can make miracles fall from the sky, but we will prevail."

Sydney let herself contemplate for only one moment. "I'll give you half tomorrow morning, half when we get the injunction reversed."

"That's fair. I like your style, young lady. The Crawfords are in for the shock of their lives."

"Good," Sydney said. "How are we going to do it?"

"Media, of course. Come to work tomorrow dressed to be on TV."

"TV?" Sydney's breath caught in her throat. Since she was ten, the only time she'd seen her mother was when she'd been on TV. She was now fighting the same battle her mother had fought.

"Got a problem with it, Sydney? I can understand if you don't want to be in the limelight, but you can only help your cause by standing up for it."

Sydney nodded, her phone beeping, letting her know she had only a little bit of battery life left.

Merry had done it. "Not a problem. What time?"

"Ten A.M. We want to make the noon news. Get a good night's sleep."

The phone clicked in Sydney's hand, and the rest of her questions blew away.

Merry had done it. Sydney saw her mother with her bright smile and beautiful curls that cascaded around her shoulders. She'd always clipped the vibrant ringlets back when they would make bread, and then she'd pull Sydney's hair back, too. They'd sprinkle the ingredients on wax paper and start kneading.

Sydney's eyes closed.

"Like this. Just like Mama's. Very good! You're going to be an expert in no time."

Sydney would knead until her little hands cramped. *"Just like you, Mommy."*

She wished her mother were here now.

The thought didn't bother her as it once would have.

During those interviews, Merry had always been proud and intelligent. Her confidence had sparkled, and she'd carried herself like a winner.

Sydney pointed her car toward home to prepare. She would be no less.

She slowed at her normal exit and directed her car to his house.

She needed to cross one more item off her to-do list.

10

"How could you? I told you no!"

Sydney's stomach jumped at the weight of anger in her father's voice. He stalked around the living room, his feet never leaving the plastic runners. If he could, he would Saran Wrap his house just to keep the inside sterile.

It was ironic that her father made his living as a maintenance man. His job was to clean up dirt. And he was good at it. But somehow the project he felt gave him the most respectability had become tainted. All by the woman he'd once loved, then wiped from his life. And there wasn't anything he could do about it.

"I understand your shock, Dad, but this is something I want to do."

"I forbid you—"

"You can't tell me what to do anymore," she said

firmly. "I'm a grown woman, and I'm the owner of FLIRT."

"Do you know what this will do to my good name? All your life I thought of you. Why can't you show me that same respect?"

Sydney understood her father's anger, but they weren't living in the olden days when something like this would shame the family. These were the days of instant media. It was sad, but everyone lived in a glass house.

She sat forward, wanting to calm his fears. "Dad, I've always respected you, but this doesn't have anything to do with you. She left me the store. I want to run it or at least try. I'd hoped you'd understand."

"You're selfish and materialistic, just like her. The coat I bought you wasn't good enough anymore?"

The sense of dishonor that washed over her shook the foundation of her decision to open FLIRT, and for a split second she wanted to be her father's little girl again and please him.

But the shame that glinted from his eyes was an ocean deep. Backing down would forever keep her a servant to her father's will.

"There are other businesses you could pursue, Sydney. We could open a cleaning company together. You'd run the office, and I'd hire the staff and manage the workers. Now that's honorable work."

Sydney couldn't think of anything less appealing.

It wasn't that she thought she was too good, but cleaning was backbreaking, hard work that offered no advancement and no opportunity to change. Besides, she didn't want to work for her father. Living on her own had shown her the freedoms she'd never known.

She wasn't willing to give that up just to assuage her father's desire for control.

Owning FLIRT was something she wanted. The first thing she'd wanted that didn't jibe with her father's dreams.

Rising from the plastic-covered couch, she pulled her purse onto her shoulder. "Dad, when I was about to turn thirteen, I planned this huge party; then there was this outbreak of tuberculosis at school. They closed school for three days. We all had to be tested, and on the weekend of my thirteenth birthday, nobody came to my party. Do you remember what you said to me?"

He barely nodded. "What's that got to do with anything?"

"You told me as hard as it was for me to believe, the world didn't revolve around me."

"What's your point?"

Sydney walked to the front door. "I'm giving you your words back."

"You do this and you leave me no choice—I'll disown you."

Sydney winced as a sharp pain radiated through her chest.

"Don't do this," she begged, her eyes filling with tears. "Don't make me choose."

"Girl, I've lived my life for you. I've raised you into a woman. If you go against me, you will not be my child. You'll be as dead as her."

Tears streamed down her cheeks as she looked at her father.

"Did you disown her, too? Did you stop her from seeing me?"

"Everything I did was for you. She didn't deserve your innocence. She would have tainted you."

"Dad! She was my mother."

"And she didn't choose you. She chose the worldly life that didn't amount to anything. She died alone. That's what happens when you walk away from your family. Is that what you want?"

"Dad, you're breaking my heart."

"Don't make me, Sydney. Give this up and we can go back to the way we were."

"Don't ask me. Please."

The tear that slid from his eye ran through the grooves of fury on his face, leaving nothing to run off his chin while her tears splattered the wooden foyer floor they'd laid together fifteen years ago.

"You do this, you're dead to me. In or out, either way, close the door."

Her father walked into the kitchen, leaving her alone.

Sydney wanted to beg him to take the words back, but she couldn't.

Making the second decision of her adult life alone, Sydney stepped onto the porch and pulled the door closed behind her.

11

"Sorry, but I can't work for you. Drew, I have a reputation to uphold. How long do you think you're going to stay in business adjacent to a sex shop?"

Drew looked at the Armani-clad, waif-thin, bespectacled maitre d', whose crossed legs bumped the underside of the table, and wanted to strangle him.

"We have a contract, Eugene."

The trendy maitre d' looked at Drew with savvy blue eyes. "My lawyers have already found a loophole. This place was perfect until Madam X was resurrected. Unfortunately, the writing is on the wall, and I can't go down with a sinking ship. Sor-ry," he sang.

Drew felt as if another long thread in his perfectly woven tapestry had unraveled.

He needed Eugene. The man had contacts in the restaurant world that had been useful in helping Drew get started. He'd counted on Eugene's marketing skills to get the word out to critics and reporters so that Satisfaction would get reviewed.

Eugene had even used his exclusive A-list and booked those clients for reservations during the first month of business.

The mayor and governor were among the VIPs, along with company presidents, CFOs, dignitaries and athletes from the metro Atlanta area.

Drew had used family connections to invite Atlanta's old money. They were sold out for four months. But today alone, he'd already processed ten cancellations. He had the feeling that trend would continue.

Drew kept the TV on mute as Lori King and her client continued their carnival of a press conference. He didn't really need the TV; he only had to look out the windows at the jam-packed parking lot to see the circus.

He strode around, frustrated. "Satisfaction is the hottest restaurant opening in Atlanta."

"Past tense," Eugene said with a smirk that could only be pulled off by the gayest of men.

Drew didn't care about his sexual affiliation. The man was a damn fine maitre d'.

"*Would* have been. I can't get the mayor or the governor in here now. They're not the moneymakers. The people who want to be seen with them, *that's* how we make our money. But having that store open lowers everybody's worth. *Perception*, Drew. Our city officials want to eat at classy, expensive establishments so they can be seen by the influential and prominent *as* influential and prominent."

His hands flapped out. "Get it? After their tiramisu,

they don't want to give a press conference about the sex shop next door. I nor they want to touch that hot button with a ten-foot pole. Sorry, Drew."

This was exactly what he'd feared. Drew crossed his arms and nodded. "Have your attorneys contact my attorneys and we'll get you processed out."

Eugene looked relieved. "Best of luck to you."

The man walked swiftly from the restaurant. Drew watched him walk up the drive, hop into a Mercedes coupe and drive away from the melee. He'd had the forethought to park for an easy escape.

Drew wiped his face and walked back over to the mounted TV and pressed the volume button.

"The injunction was illegally obtained. We are in compliance in every way." Lori King glared at the camera, daring a reporter to contradict her.

A young man who hadn't bothered with a winter coat thrust his microphone forward. "The order states that an adult store can't operate within a mile of a church. As you know, Tabernacle Baptist is being constructed nearly a mile away. Therefore you're out of compliance. How do you respond?"

Lori played to the young reporter, turning slightly so the entire sign, in multicolored letters, blazed behind her. "FLIRT has been a fixture in this community for five years and in Atlanta for more than two decades. That church broke ground a month ago."

Drew sat down, his arms crossed.

"But the law is clear. An adult store can't open within a mile of the church."

Lori's smile was grand. "That's not how I read the law."

"And what's your interpretation?" the aggressive young reporter asked Sydney.

Drew blinked in astonishment. Sydney looked gorgeous all made up with her hair curled, and her pink coat adding feminine touches that accentuated the beauty that God had given her.

"They can't open within a mile of us," she said.

The crowd became animated, and Drew felt his stomach sink to his feet. King was crazy.

"That's rather brazen, don't you think, Ms. Morris? A house of worship—"

"Is a tax-paying business in this community," Lori broke in, effectively turning the attention back to her. She held up a document. "We've received an injunction to halt construction on the church until the city council can rule on the violation of the ordinance."

The reporters jostled each other, fighting for microphone space.

"Your arms aren't too short to box with God, Ms. King?"

Lori stepped forward, the cameras closing in on her. "My belief in God has nothing to do with this legal action. Ms. Morris's mother Merry died three weeks ago, leaving her the business. There was never a lapse in ownership of FLIRT, which is what the injunction stipulates. On that basis alone, the injunction against us is invalid. They will rule in our favor in the subsequent action because FLIRT was already in existence and operating before the church broke ground. I assure you, we are in compliance."

"And the church construction?"

"Will have to cease. All of this legal maneuvering has

been initiated by the powerful Crawford family. They've decided to suck up real estate in this area like they did in East Atlanta, and they think they can shove small businesses out. We're here to say we will not be bullied."

Drew wiped his mouth, bracing himself. King had just pulled the entire family into the fight. He hadn't expected that.

The door to the restaurant opened, and his cousins Mike and Julian walked in. "So you've heard. We need to have a meeting," Julian said.

"I didn't expect this." Drew stood and shook their hands. They pulled up chairs to finish watching the press conference.

"Lori King is an amazing attorney," Julian commented, his unflappable demeanor making Drew nervous. "You should have talked to me before seeking that injunction."

"We were within our rights," Mike argued. "I went to the city council and met in a closed-door session. Once I was able to prove the zoning violation, they saw enough evidence and made their ruling. It was perfectly legal."

"If her facts are correct, then you're between a rock and a hard place. She's going to use that church to break you down," Julian said.

"What are you talking about?" Mike demanded.

"If Sydney owned the store as they said, the church is out of compliance and has to move. They've already broken ground. What's the chance of that happening?"

Mike sprang to his feet. "She didn't own the store. She wasn't in possession of the property. She didn't sign the papers until a few days ago."

"That's a very fine hair to hinge your business on.

"What happens when the decision is reversed? And it will be," Julian asked quietly, watching his brother.

Drew watched Mike, too, for the first time wondering if they'd made a mistake.

"It won't," Mike said, smacking his palm with his fist.

"Again, you should have checked with me before you went off half-cocked, Mike. Now she's dragged the family into this fight. How's that make us look?"

Mike swore, and Drew knew Julian was right. He wanted to curse, but didn't. His entire life savings was invested in the restaurant. He had to open. He had to succeed.

Drew dropped his head. "What's the worst case?"

"The proverbial shit has hit the fan, guys. Lori King is seeking publicity. You brought the church into this. Big mistake. Now they have to answer the injunction against them. That's going to cost them money, and they aren't going to be happy."

"But I bought this spot when FLIRT was closed for business. I was told it was never going to open again," Drew argued. "I'm sure they were told the same thing."

Julian shook his head. "Both businesses proceeded with bad information. Merry Morris had been sick, and her business had been closed, but there was an heir who legally exercised her right to operate the business she inherited. Have you considered buying her out?"

"She turned me down."

Mike walked to the farthest corner of the restaurant and watched the press conference from the window.

"Sweeten the offer," Julian advised.

"She won't bite," Drew said.

"She sounds like a true Crawford woman." Julian chuckled.

Mike and Drew glanced at each other, but Drew wasn't going there. "What's the worst case?"

"Mike?" Julian said.

"The church won't open, and Lori King and FLIRT get all the free publicity they desire, but she also gets to open her store right next to your restaurant. The family suffers a little bad publicity for trying to squash small businesses, mistreating women and being prejudiced."

"Crap," Drew exhaled. He knew. This tornado was getting bigger than he'd imagined. Drew looked at Mike's back and saw the defeat in his shoulders.

"FLIRT is an institution in this county, and like it or not, you're going to have to learn how to play nice."

"I just lost my maitre d' and ten reservations. Playing nice is costing me big-time."

"Find a way to make it work. Twenty years ago my father sat on the city council that gave Merry Morris the right to be here. If you think you're going to reverse that, you'd have a better chance of moving Labor Day to January. Work something out," Julian told Drew and his brother. "Or else you'll have more than me telling you you're wrong. I've got to go. The twins have a cheerleader competition."

Julian got to the door and turned around.

"What?" Drew wondered what other bad news his cousin had to impart.

"Don't take too long. The elders in the family shouldn't have to deal with this."

Drew nodded, and Julian left. Mike walked over and took his seat. "Man, I'm sorry. I didn't know about my father having sat on the board."

Drew was sure the same ramifications that ran through his head were going through Mike's as well. "You're supposed to have my back. You should have known."

"I know."

Anger coursed through Drew at Mike and himself. He'd never played the odds when he worked under-cover. He'd underestimated civilian life. And it was costing him.

"So Eugene quit," Mike said.

Drew nodded. "Yep. This is going downhill fast."

Mike's gaze became speculative. "The city council isn't meeting again until February sixth. What if we enter into preliminary negotiations with King and her client, and then hold out on making a decision?"

Drew glared at him. "You've got to be kidding. We don't have a leg to stand on, and we've jeopardized a church's opening."

"Focus," Mike said sternly. "The church will have to figure their way out of this themselves. Once FLIRT opened and the congregation found out, this would have come up anyway, believe me. What I'm trying to tell you is that Sydney Morris has only so much money and so much time. If our strategy is to negotiate and hold, we've got her."

Trying to destroy Sydney had already backfired.

Drew tried not to think about her pink Burberry boots and the look of fear on her face the last time he'd seen her. "I'll give it one more try. Set up a meeting for next week and we'll make them an offer."

12

Sydney reread the chapter on tax preparation and wiped her eyes with the damp washcloth that she'd kept by her side for the last two days. Her eyes burned, and her chest felt as if an eighteen-wheeler had stalled between her third and fourth rib.

The silence of the cold February night was broken only by her hiccupping sob.

She couldn't stop crying.

She wanted to lie down and let grief have its way—then maybe she could sleep—but grief was greedy. It was almost as if it wanted to dissect her molecular structure and re-create itself as the source of her life, and a few times Sydney almost gave in. She wanted to, but something kept her from the edge of grief's cliff.

It wasn't pride, or fear, or even faith that tomorrow would bring a brand-new day.

Sydney wiped her tears and slapped the pages of the

book on her lap. She couldn't identify what kept her reading, taking notes, testing herself and pushing physical limits her body had never experienced before.

Perhaps it was her sense of survival, but Sydney wasn't sure. She just had to keep on.

Clenching her fists, she made herself not pick up the white cordless phone and dial her father's number again. She wouldn't call anymore or leave another tearful plea for him to meet her halfway.

He'd kept his word for two days and had ended their relationship. And although she prayed it wouldn't last, a painful premonition in the back of her mind whispered what she wouldn't consciously acknowledge. He meant to cut her out of his life as he had her mother.

Her dad was the only family she had besides her friendship with Evette and her family. Her father had to take her back.

Tears sprinkled the pages, and Sydney wiped the stubborn flow. She had to stop crying or her head would surely burst.

Standing, she looked around at the mess she'd accumulated, a testimony to her hard work. By rote she cleaned up and dropped the popcorn bowl in the sink and her Coke cans in the recycle bin. Back in the living room, she stretched out on the floor. Fatigue called out to her, and she bargained with herself. If she stopped crying, she could rest for fifteen minutes.

Sighing, Sydney closed her eyes and thought she'd quiz herself on tax law, but instead, she saw Merry.

The picture Lori had given her was the image Sydney dreamed of. A smiling mother who was alive and twirled her young daughter around. They both laughed gleefully, dressed in matching white dresses with pink ribbons on the front. They were playing hide-and-seek in a grove of fescue green grass, butterflies fluttering amid the wildflowers.

Sydney gestured for her mother to stay while she hid behind a tree and counted to ten. She ran, and her mother chased her all the way back to the blanket where they collapsed in a fit of giggles.

Merry picked dandelions and gave one to Sydney and told her to close her eyes and make a wish. Sydney wished, and when she opened her eyes, she blew on her dandelion and watched the pollen float on the warm breeze.

She looked around for her mother, but Merry had disappeared. Sydney could still hear her laughter. It burrowed into her chest, becoming one with her heartbeat. Sydney wasn't afraid. Her mother was still with her.

The temperature changed, and a cool breeze caressed her cheek. She looked down. The grass was gone, in its place were the feet of a woman in strappy sandals. In the distance she could see Merry, who blew her a kiss goodbye. Sydney reached out to stop her, but the kiss slid up her fingertips, over her hand and arm, before claiming her whole body in a warm embrace. Sydney lowered her hand, satisfied.

Warmth surrounded her, and she reached out and felt a man's jacket slide over her arms. She knew it was a man's because of the alluring aroma of aftershave and cologne. She welcomed the comfort and looked up at the generous stranger.

Drew looked down at her. With a deliberateness that belied his strength, he took her into his arms.

When her head was resting in the bend of his arm, his right hand wrapped around her waist, and he bent his head and claimed her mouth in a kiss so tender, if it hadn't been so sweet it would have broken her heart.

They were adversaries. Enemies. But his kiss took her to a dimension where there was only pleasure. He groaned with wanting, and she enticed him by making her body meet his.

His mustache brushed her lips, bringing Sydney up on her toes.

Drew didn't have a mustache.

Sydney's eyes popped open, the phone by her head ringing. She fought her way out of the darkness and came to her knees. Somehow in her sleep, she'd pulled the blanket off the couch and had covered her head with it.

The carpet had been Drew's mustache. Embarrassment flooded her as she answered the phone. "Yes?"

"Turn on the TV," the caller said. "You're back in the news and will stay there until you get out of our town and stay out."

Fully awake, and alarmed, Sydney hung up the phone and fumbled through the books and papers on the couch and floor until she found the remote. She flicked on the TV and was shocked to see a line of picketing protesters in front of FLIRT and her house.

"The owner of the store is Sydney Morris. She's thirty one and she lives in Atlanta. She's a porn peddler! she insists upon opening this hole of sin and invading our lives with this smut, we think the public should know all about her. We're here to protest this attempt to erode our society, and we're not leaving!"

Her mouth fell open as the man rattled off her street address and home phone number.

Scared, she looked outside, then ran to the back of her house and into her bedroom. The sight of her front lawn had alarmed her. Should she leave? Call the police? She didn't know what to do. Her instincts told her to pack and get out of the house as quickly as possible.

She dialed the police. "Nine-one-one operator. What's your emergency?"

"My name is Sydney Morris, and there are reporters and other people outside my home to harass me because I own an adult store in Atlanta."

"What's your emergency?"

"There are crazy people outside my house!"

"Ma'am, if they're not doing anything, we can't get involved."

Pounding started on her front door, shaking the glass.

Sydney screamed. "Do you hear that? These aren't peaceful protesters. These are people who intend me harm. Can you at least give me an escort off my property to somewhere safe?"

"I'll send a squad car."

"Thank you," Sydney said in relief. "Wait. What precinct will they be from?"

"Twelve."

"Thank you so much."

"Ms. Morris, be ready to leave when they get there."

"Okay."

Dropping the phone on the base, Sydney ran to the garage, pulled her large suitcase off the wire shelf and groaned at the layer of dust coating the surface. She

didn't have time to clean it or go through her norma
travel checklist. Leaving was all that mattered.

Hurrying back into the bedroom, dragging the sui
case behind her, she tore through her drawers and pile
neat rows of underwear and socks into the bottom o
the case, then jeans and sweaters.

On top of her clothes, she tossed in her toiletries an
zipped up the bag.

Maybe I'm overreacting, she thought and slowed dow

*They'll leave when they don't get a response, and this who
thing will blow over.*

Taking two deep breaths, she dropped her hands t
her hips and jumped at the pounding on the front doo
Instead of going through the foyer, she tiptoed into th
garage and stood on the bumper of her car to see ou
the small window at the top of the garage door.

News vans blocked her neighbor's sidewalk, reporte
were walking up her driveway and a carload of picketer
spilled into the street.

A hysterical scream burst from her mouth before sh
covered it and got down. How would the police rescu
her? She had to get out of her house on her own.

Rushing inside, she grabbed her purse and keys, bu
didn't know what to do next. If she left alone, they'
follow. If she stayed, they'd harass her to death. She wa
trapped.

A knock at the back door startled her, and sh
picked up an empty glass vase to defend herself.

A female police officer stood on the back deck an
gestured her to the door, her badge up.

Relief flooded Sydney, and she hurried over and l
the woman in.

"I'm so glad to see you. I'm being bombarded. Can you get them to leave?"

"No." The green-eyed woman looked around cautiously and then whistled out the door. "You can call me Asia. I was sent to pick you up."

Sydney detected an air of mystery to the woman, but couldn't put her finger on what wasn't right. "You're arresting me?"

"No. More like a rescue." Two additional women materialized like the breeze off the ocean. They looked remarkably similar, with their penetrating gray eyes, bone structure and lean figures.

"Who are they?"

Asia responded. "This is Africa and Europe. Africa will pretend to be you. She's going to stay here, and they will go out the front door while you and I go out the back, hopefully to safety."

"Wow." Sydney watched as the woman Africa pulled a wig from inside her coat that resembled the way Sydney styled her hair. Europe took the vase from Sydney's hands and put it back in its rightful place.

"You look almost like me. It's uncanny." Sydney couldn't help but stare.

"That's the point," Europe said, her gaze darting to the foyer. "Where's your coat?"

"I'll get it." Sydney said and was stopped.

"Just tell me and I'll get it. You take my jacket. Asia," she said to the uniformed cop, "we'll rendezvous at nineteen hundred hours."

Sydney pulled on her shoes, the jacket and got her purse. "My suitcase."

Asia stopped her. "You can't take it. Right now it'
about you getting out unnoticed. If you have a bag
that's a dead giveaway. Give Africa your house keys."

For the first time, Sydney felt unsure. "What precinc
are you from?"

"Twelve," Asia responded curtly. All three wome
looked at their watches. "Let's move—now."

Sydney was taken by the arm to the back door, a ha
placed on her head, and the jacket Africa had given t
her slipped on her body and zipped to the neck.

"Move when I move. Keep your head down. Act nat
ural. If anyone stops us, you keep moving regardless o
what I do."

"Where are we going?"

"Someplace safe. Right now, to a black Explorer :
block from here. We're cutting through the woods, s
get ready. Now!"

Before Sydney could think twice she was hustled ou
of her house and across her backyard. There was onl
maybe fifty or sixty feet of space between her house an
the woods, but it seemed like a mile.

She did as she was told and stepped when Asia steppe
and stopped when the woman threw up her hand. The
trek to the Explorer seemed to take forever. Their rout
was circuitous and somewhat difficult given that a ligh
icy rain had started to fall.

Sydney felt every stab of rain against her cheeks, bu
she didn't complain as Asia seemed immune to the ele
ments. She never lost her footing on the uneven ter
rain, and she never slowed. Finally their feet hit cemen
and they continued on the sidewalk.

"Easy," Asia ordered, smiling at her. A news truc

110

rushed past, and the driver did a double take. "Don't look back! Hug me like we're saying goodbye."

Sydney did as she was told, praying the truck would keep going. She couldn't tell, though. She was facing away from the traffic.

"He turned on your street. Get in fast!"

The back passenger door opened, and Sydney jumped in. "Lie down!" Asia ordered, and Sydney obeyed.

The SUV started, and they eased into traffic. "Can I get up now?"

"Not until we get to safety. Two news vans just passed us. We're going to take the long way. Just get comfortable. You're going to be there for a while."

"Where are we going?"

"We have a quiet location about an hour from here where you can get your bearings and decide what you'd like to do. Unless you'd like to go to a relative's house?"

"No!" She wasn't welcome at her father's. "The safe house is fine."

Sydney's heart pounded with fear. Two weeks ago her life had been so normal it would have put an elderly person to sleep, and now she was being spirited away from her quiet house by cops named after continents.

All for owning an adult toy store.

Who knew life would be so interesting.

Sydney tried to count the minutes that passed, but lost track as the tires created a steady thrum against the wet road. Between the tires and windshield wipers, she was lulled into a relaxed state.

She didn't realize they'd stopped until she heard Asia's voice. "The eagle has landed."

Am I the eagle? Sydney wondered distantly.

"Sydney, it's safe to get up now."

The pitch-black night greeted her when she glance
out the window. No stars covered the sky. Rain pep
pered the SUV in a steady beat that sounded like hors
hooves. Sydney stretched, and the back door opened
She had no idea where she was. Only hoped it was nic
enough for her to take a hot bath.

The back seemed vaguely familiar, but she couldn
place it. Disoriented, she hurried into the darkene
hallway and knew the familiar smell.

"Thanks, Jade."

Was that Drew?

"Don't worry, cuz. You'll be getting my bill."

Sydney reached out and hit the wall switch. Dre
Crawford stood with the woman cop. Only she wasn
dressed like a cop anymore. She had on a cap with lon
braids hanging down her back. What happened to he
uniform? Who were these people?

"What's going on?"

The woman cocked her head. "I'm Jade. I'm not
cop. Sorry for the deception. My job is reconnaissanc
You're safe now. Nobody followed us. Your bag will b
delivered in a day or two. Good night."

"Not a cop? You kidnapped me!"

"Did I really?" The woman's honest face mad
Sydney back down.

"Maybe that's a little strong, but who are you?"

"The good guys. Trust me, okay?" Jade squeezed he
hand and backed away, pointing at Drew. "You've got
lot of explaining to do. Behave yourself."

With that, she was gone.

Sydney regarded Drew, who stood in the back hall, a look of concern on his face. He was dressed in his typical black, his arms bulging from beneath the sleeves. This man was no chef.

"What the hell is reconnaissance? What about the two women in my house?"

"Calm down," Drew said. "Jade's my cousin's wife, and she did me a favor."

"*You a favor?* You call me being kidnapped a favor?"

Inexplicably, Sydney wanted to follow Jade.

Being with the unknown woman somehow seemed better than standing in the rear entrance of Satisfaction with Drew.

"I know you have questions, and I'll answer every one. I fixed dinner. Why don't we eat and talk?"

He walked off, leaving Sydney alone. She opened the back door and looked out. The SUV she'd arrived in was gone, and she didn't have a car.

The cold air, rain and ice slanted down from the Atlanta sky and smacked the concrete surface. It was almost beautiful, but its simplistic beauty was deceptive.

Tomorrow the black ice would wreak havoc on the roads and would be the cause of many accidents.

"We could eat outside, but it's warmer in here."

Drew was behind her, speaking softly as if he were trying to sweet-talk her. Sydney kept the door ajar.

It's too dangerous to leave, her brain informed her.

"Why'd you do this?" she asked him.

"I felt guilty." A white mug appeared over her shoulder, and Sydney sniffed the cocoa. The fear was almost gone, but she had to admit, she was still a bit unsettled by Drew.

In or out. The words reverberated in her head. Rain splattered her face, and she stepped back. She'd spent the better part of the last two days studying and crying, feeling sorry for herself. Now she could get some answers and put some concerns to rest.

She closed the door and locked it. Turning, she accepted the mug. "Who are you? You're not really a chef. You're some kind of spy or something, and if you don't give me the truth, I'll have you arrested for kidnapping."

13

Drew considered himself to be a reasonable man, sound and practical. He'd been in tough situations where he'd had to rely strictly upon his instincts or his life would have ended violently.

He'd known when to offer a bribe and when to fight with his fists. Now, facing Sydney, a woman he hardly knew, he wanted to throw up his hands in defeat.

The feeling was so extraordinarily opposite to anything he'd ever experienced, Drew wasn't sure how to proceed.

Right now, he wished a man had a gun to his head. The decision to kill or be killed was quite simple.

"I'm going to eat. You're welcome to join me." He left her at the back door, a part of him wishing she'd walk off into the freezing rain. But then he'd go after her; that was his M.O.

Silence yawned long and deep. He heard the whisper of her breath several feet away. She'd come inside. A small step in his favor, though not one he'd celebrate.

"Where's the ladies' room?"

Her voice stroked his back, but not as he liked from a woman. The usual softer melody was painted with weighty anger. He should be used to it by now, but this situation was different. He wasn't accustomed to being the bad guy.

"Straight back and to the left."

Sydney stared him down. Her eyes promised that the fight would be good.

"I'll be here when you get back."

"That's what I'm afraid of," she said and walked off.

Drew could feel the rhythm of his heartbeat escalate until it was racing. A minute passed. Two.

Would she leave through the ladies' room window and turn him in to the police, or would she give him the opportunity to explain and perhaps fix this mess?

He'd never known the cloying suffocation of anxiety, how it seeped over you like quicksand, but he had a taste of it now, and Drew mentally headed in the opposite direction.

He knew what he had to do. He had to start by feeding her.

In the kitchen, he pulled out dinner.

The appetizers were already cold, but that didn't matter. Nothing about today had gone perfectly. He poured wine into stemmed glasses and took them to the table.

Pointing the remote, he fired up two of the four gas fireplaces, lit the hurricane candle centerpiece, but decided against music. He didn't want Sydney to think he'd planned a kidnapping *and* a romantic evening.

Working quickly, he dressed the plates and had everything ready when she reappeared. Attuned to her more deeply than he cared to acknowledge, he knew she was behind him before she cleared her throat.

"Go ahead and sit," he said. "I'll be just a minute more."

Drew grabbed their plates, turned and faced the defiant, angry woman. She looked ready to burst, her golden eyes storming, her finger aimed at his chest. He braced himself.

"I don't appreciate your interference in my life. You had me kidnapped! I believed she was a cop. I'd just called the police because reporters and those crazy people with their sick signs had converged on my neighborhood. Do you know how afraid I was? I trusted her."

"Sydney, this was between us. I didn't expect them to go to your house. When I saw that, I had to step in." Drew put the plates down and moved toward her.

Her eyes showed the strain of the ordeal. He hated to think he'd put the stress lines on her beautiful face. The closer he got, the tearier her eyes became until two spilled over and streaked her cheeks. He backed up a step. He hadn't expected tears.

"I'm a single woman, Drew. I live alone. I trusted them. She could have been a killer. I could have disappeared, and nobody that cares about me—" She stopped then, her throat working up and down in an effort not to cry. "Nobody would have known how to find me. I feel so stupid."

The tumbled words rang in his ears, and he finally

understood the depths of her fear. In the name of help-ing her, he'd about frightened her to death.

"No." She punched Drew in the shoulder as he tried to pull Sydney to him.

He held his hands up, wishing he'd done things dif-ferently. "This is my fault," he said. "I was only thinking of getting you out of there. I was stupid. Sydney," he said, softly. "I'm sorry you were scared. I'm sorry."

She covered her face with her hands. He didn't hurt from her hitting him, but he didn't want to make an-other mistake by touching her. If he gave her some space and walked away, she might think he didn't appreciate the impact having her forcibly removed from her house had on her.

For the first time in recent memory, Drew was vul-nerable.

"Why are you still looking at me?"

Drew glanced around the kitchen, then met Sydney's wet gaze. "At this point, I don't know what to do."

Surprise registered in the depths of her red-rimmed eyes.

"I find it hard to believe you don't know how to handle a crying woman."

He looked off to the side, then smiled at her, hoping the storm had abated, at least for the time being. Sydney's face was pale, and she looked drawn and tired. He pulled a cotton napkin from the drawer, folded it and gently dabbed her tears.

"Do you accept my apology?"

Drew was holding his breath, he realized.

Sydney didn't draw away, but she didn't look at him either. "I'm thinking about it."

"What do I have to do to convince you?"

"What have you done in the past?"

"It depends. If I was trying to apologize to my little sister who's twelve, I'd kiss and tickle her until she forgave me."

She looked out the corner of her eye at him. "You don't seem the type to have a sister."

Her remark caught him off guard. He'd expected her to say something about not kissing or touching *her*. "You're right. I was born to wolves. The family adopted me and made me into the half man I am. You can blame my parents for my poor upbringing."

Drew watched her closely, hoping she'd forgive him just a little. He was working harder at this apology than any other in his life.

Finally her cheek moved, and the tiniest of smiles ghosted her lips before it was gone.

"What else?" she asked, her hands folded in front of her.

He got a little closer. "If I were apologizing to a woman, I'd buy flowers or I'd cook for her. And if it was really a big apology, I might do all of the above and then some."

"I'm hungry."

Some of the tension eased from his shoulders. Good. Hungry he understood.

Another tear escaped, and she swiped at it with quick fingers. The spray sprinkled his lips, and he was swept with the urge to fold her in his arms. He couldn't help but think there was more to the tears, more to the overwhelming sadness surrounding her.

Then he remembered that her mother had just died.

And her life had been thrust into the limelight. For even the most seasoned public figure, unexpected media attention was hard to manage, but for a novice, these had to be some of the most challenging days of her life.

Drew took a chance and reached for her hand. "Are you going to hit me again?" he asked, trying to lighten the mood and, he realized, make friends with her.

The tip of her tongue rested on her lower lip before going home. A myriad of emotions crossed her face, the last being regret. "No," she said softly. "Can I have something to drink?"

He felt a stirring in his chest that broadcast throughout his torso, ending in his thigh. An image of Sydney naked, resting inside his thighs, hit him.

This awake fantasizing had happened before during long gaps of time between intimate contact, but only with women he'd made love with in the past.

How easy would it be to run his hand down her face and press his lips into her cheek before claiming her mouth?

Drew considered the possibility, but warned himself not to touch her. Not even if she landed in his lap.

Tucking her hand in his arm, he led her to the booth he'd prepared and guided her inside.

"You like wine?" he asked, hoping he'd find something they could share in common besides not wanting to own adjacent real estate.

"Yes, but I haven't eaten in hours. I should eat something first."

He moved a glass of wine in front of her. "Sip. I'll be back with everything."

Drew warmed their food and, in the meantime, brought her water, bread and olive oil.

He set everything up on the table across from the booth and sat down opposite her.

"What is this?" she asked, staring at the plate, sipping her wine.

"Glazed shrimp for appetizers. Beef tenderloin and mixed vegetables for the entrée, and dried cherry tart for dessert, if I'm not in jail by then."

She looked him in the eye and didn't smile. "Then it better be good."

A chuckle rumbled up his chest. The woman was made of nerves he'd never seen before. They ate in silence, the steady click of silverware on fine china the soprano to the underlying bass beat of icy rain on the rooftop.

January was dying a slow and painful death, and February didn't seem to want to start much better.

He noticed how she ate and could tell that she liked the food. Once, he caught her nodding to herself, and he took that as confirmation that she was enjoying what she was eating. He served the beef tenderloin and had sat back down when she lifted her wine and sipped.

"Who are you?" Sydney asked.

Drew chewed his food, giving himself a moment to analyze the impact a truthful answer could have on her.

"Before I retired, I was essentially a bodyguard for people who needed protection. I worked for the bureau for twenty years until I was shot last year. I retired and bought Satisfaction."

"The bureau meaning the FBI?"

"Yes."

"They wouldn't let you keep your job and work in another capacity?"

"That was an impractical option."

"Why?" Sydney asked the question as if staying was the obvious choice.

"Things changed."

Drew didn't think he could explain fear to a woman who'd probably never held a gun before. He'd done his job for twenty years, slipping into the lives of others and manipulating them to keep them from danger. But once he'd gotten shot, he could no longer perform his duties in secret. His cover had been blown, and instead of rescuing, he'd had to be rescued.

Ultimately, Drew had been proud of himself. He hadn't been like some of the old codgers who had to practically be thrown out the door. He'd retired the day after his twenty-year anniversary.

Satisfaction was his plan B.

And the threat to his livelihood sat across from him savoring beef tenderloin.

Drew dragged his gaze away and ate. Watching her filled him up in a different way.

"Is Asia in law enforcement?"

Drew nodded, wanting to keep a dialogue open until Sydney was comfortable. "You could say that."

"There were two women with her. They looked—" A puzzled expression crossed her face. She put her wineglass down, and he refilled it. "Like they were related to you."

"My cousins. Trina and probably Tracy."

"So law enforcement runs in your entire family?"

"A bit," he said, elusive. Sharing the Crawford legacy

required history between two people and a half case of wine.

As a maintenance lover to his women friends, he saw to it they didn't get personal. Well, not beyond sharing what felt good sexually. This was new territory for him. One he wasn't altogether comfortable with.

"I've read about the famous Crawford family," Sydney said. "They're doctors, dentists, ambassadors, and lawyers, and, oh, singers. I forgot about Lauren"—Sydney sipped her wine—"I forgot her last name. How many times removed are you from them?"

Drew topped off their glasses. His father and uncle Julian were brothers, and while Uncle Julian was the hotshot judge, Drew was proud that his father had made his living in good old-fashioned farming. He was recently acknowledged to be the largest private owner of farmland in the state.

"Those Crawfords are my first cousins."

"They're aggressive businessmen. I was told they won't be denied. I don't find that so hard to believe. Not after getting to know Asia and her bat girls. The deception was extraordinary. How do I know that anything you say is true?"

"I'm not lying now."

She looked him over with eyes that were going dreamy. The wine was working into her system. "I want to believe you, but I don't."

Loose lips, he thought. They were dragging on his heartstrings.

"The family owns businesses in the Atlanta area, but we're no different from anyone else. We can't take the law into our own hands."

Sydney finished her food. "Sure you can," she said agreeably. She pushed her hair from her face and re-adjusted the front of her shirt. Her tongue darted out again, and Drew wished for the first time in his that if he could come back reincarnated, he'd return as a set of lips. "You Crawfords are trying to shut me down. You should learn how to fight fair."

She was getting drunk, and tomorrow, that'd be his fault, too.

Drew took their plates to the kitchen and brought back dessert, moving her wineglass out of reach. She reached past him and picked it up.

"I thought I was being fair," Drew said, sitting across from her. "I offered you a settlement, and you turned me down."

"You sicced your attorney on me, and now my doors are shut, but don't worry. I won't hold the protesters against you. You were just helping me out. Then there's the whole kidnapping thing. You've been so fair, the hatchet in my back, I hardly feel it."

Drew put down his napkin and moved to her side of the booth. "Sydney, look at me."

She rested her head against the back of the booth. Turning, a lock of hair fell across her cheek. When she opened her eyes, their smoky depths captured his.

"I already apologized."

"I accept," she said, surprising him. Suddenly the anger was gone. "You made me food and I ate it. I don't have an ugly nature," she explained. "You apologized and I accepted."

Drew looked at the half-drunk woman and knew she was just a second from being kissed so thoroughly, they

124

could be thrust into a different time zone from the power of his desire for her.

Longing had crept into him. He took her hand in his; their fingers laced when she flipped their hands over and drew her nails down his palm. A thousand tendrils of wanting rushed up his legs, and his fingers snapped closed around hers.

"You want me to close for good?" she asked him.

He looked up at her, then at their hands, and he couldn't help himself. "Yes."

"I have too much to lose." Her eyes rested on his mouth. The whispered words danced on his lips.

"You're going to ruin me." He leaned into her.

"God, you're gorgeous."

"I was thinking the same about you."

Before he could reconsider, Drew tipped her chin and kissed her.

The softness of her lips against his welcomed him to a place he'd never been. Her tongue met his in a tentative greeting, and he thought she'd pull back, this kiss taking them to a foreign land.

When she didn't, when the delicate tip of her wine-laced tongue laved his lips, Drew pulled her to him, slanted his mouth over hers and kissed her for all he was worth.

The kiss ended when her hands sought his chest and worked up to his chin.

"We're enemies," she whispered. "We can't do this."

"I don't want to fight with you. Quite the contrary. Two hundred thousand."

Their lips froze inches apart, and her eyes met his. Hooded passion faded into the golden brown tint of a fighter who wasn't going to throw the round for any reason.

"Is that your best offer?" she asked, her fingers drawing an invisible line down his chest.

"What would it take?"

"No, no, no," she said and smiled a bit, her mouth so invitingly close he couldn't help but nip at her plump bottom lip. "You offer me your very best, and then I'll think about it. Until then, neighbor, we'll remain just that. I'd better get a hotel room. I've got work to do."

Thunder cracked the sky, and the lights flickered and went out.

"Are you kidding?" Sydney seemed to be asking God if He was in the cruel joke business.

The fireplace offered the only light, and if all the hurricane candles on the tables had been lit, the restaurant, with its gold and black accents, would have looked romantic.

"I'm going home," she announced and slid out of the booth. Her legs unsteady, her hair mussed and sexy, he wanted to take her just one step farther.

Sydney fumbled in her purse and looked back at him as she dialed. "'Vette, it's me. Can you pick me up from work? Why not? The roads aren't *all* iced over."

Her eyes seduced him, and Drew rose. This wasn't happening. He was stuck with a woman he'd essentially had kidnapped. A woman, now that he'd kissed, he wanted in his bed.

He found the emergency flashlights when the generator lights blinked on.

Drew looked around the restaurant that was bathed in a warm glow from the lights that had been mounted high on the walls on pedestals and was pleased. At least something was working right.

After explaining where she was, Sydney hung up the phone and came back to the table. "The roads have been closed until further notice. You're stuck with me."

"No problem. I'll walk you to your apartment. You'll be comfortable there. The reporters don't know you're here, so you can have your privacy." He picked up the jacket she'd worn and held it out for her.

"How do you know about that apartment?"

"I have one. Next door."

When she didn't move, he tilted his head down and gazed at her. "Problem?"

"Yes, as a matter of fact. That apartment belonged to my mother. I don't ever intend to go in there."

The quivering around each tersely delivered word reminded him of the temperamental Mount St. Helen. The mountain seemed sound, until she spewed ash into the sky.

Drew sensed her frailty and wanted to restore her to the sexy, kissable woman she'd been moments ago.

But they were rivals in a disagreement that would probably get uglier. Someone would lose. And Drew was determined it wasn't going to be him.

"You have two choices," he told her. "You can go to your apartment, or mine. The way I feel right now, you'd be safer there."

Sydney's head came up. "I'm going with you."

14

Sydney followed Drew to the door with the gold number one.

"I think we need to have an understanding," he said. "You still want to win, right?"

"Right."

"Then let's agree that up here where we live, this is like Switzerland, a no-fighting zone."

"Agreed," she said, looking up at him, then at the door. "Change your mind?"

"I've never been a man who let the wrong head do his thinking for him."

Heated embarrassment crept up her body. He *had* changed his mind. "I see."

Suddenly her back was against the wall, Drew's sex pressed into hers.

He kissed her then, hard and sharp, full of need. "Look at me," he said roughly.

She did and saw dark, dangerous desire in the depths of his gray eyes.

Her palms pressed into the rough surface of the walls, her body into his. He moved his hips slightly, and she rose an inch off the floor.

"You don't see that right now I'm horny as hell and I want you. You don't see the wisdom in the decision to not be with you tonight because I plied you with wine and then kissed you. You don't see tomorrow when you'll regret making love to me.

"But I do. I see it all, and damnit, before I do another thing wrong, I'm going to do this one thing right. Face your demons in your apartment, Sydney, because what's on the other side of my door, I damn sure don't want you to regret."

Need throbbed within her, yet she was aware of the darker emotion haunting her. "I'm afraid—of what I'm going to find."

"It's an apartment, baby. It can't hurt you."

His kiss whispered across her lips. He caressed her cheek with his thumb, and Sydney wanted to melt from embarrassment and unspent longing. She'd never shared her fears with anyone about not knowing her mother, but her most private pain she'd blurted to a man with whom she was embroiled in a war.

Drew now knew more than anyone. And he was her enemy. No, her rival, she amended.

Tomorrow she'd have to restore the barriers she'd erected so that she could protect herself against him and his keen ability to sway her.

But tonight, he was right. It was only an apartment, and the sooner she dealt with it, the sooner she could move on to the next phase of her life. Or she could go with Drew and face herself tomorrow. Sydney chose the greatest unknown, the one that scared her the most.

"I can't go inside if you don't let me down."

A rumble between a chuckle and a groan crawled up his chest, vibrating through hers. He leaned his head against the wall, and Sydney felt a flash of pure feminine pleasure that he was struggling so badly. He wasn't alone.

Slowly her feet touched the floor. Drew stepped away. "Where's your cell phone?"

"In my bag, why?"

"Let me see it."

Unsteady, Sydney planted her feet as she handed over the phone. "What are you doing?"

"Programming in my number. If you need anything." He placed the instrument in her palm, handed her a flashlight and backed up. "You're going to be fine."

"I don't know why you think you know everything," she said gently, grateful for his kindness.

"You're stronger than you think."

Sydney pulled the keys from her bag and looked at the one with the gold ring around it. It was the only key she hadn't found a lock to match. "Why do you say that?"

"You're here, aren't you?"

She fit the key in the chamber. "I guess I am."

"I'm right. Go in before I change my mind and take you to bed."

Sydney hesitated a long moment before opening the door that held her mother's secrets. "You go," she said,

131

looking away from his smoldering gray eyes. "I need a minute."

Drew pushed away from the wall, and she felt his finger trail along her waist as he passed. He walked to his apartment and went inside without another word.

The gold number one faced her, and she took a deep breath. Was the apartment as tacky as the store? Had her mother been a clean person? Questions flew through her mind with the speed of a hummingbird. She didn't know how to answer any of them, but she would if she took the next step.

Sydney pushed the door open and walked inside. The light switch was on the right, and she flipped it up, but was reminded that the electricity had gone off.

Swinging the flashlight, tears filled her eyes.

In the center of the table were three pictures. One of Merry and Sydney at her birth. The second was of Sydney at her third grade graduation.

The third made the tears fall from her eyes.

Merry had obviously had someone shoot the photo with a long lens and then had it digitally enhanced.

Sydney reached for the frame.

The beveled crystal was heavy, but it was her shaking hand that made the picture wobble. Sydney dropped her purse and gripped the frame firmly.

The photo was of Merry at Sydney's high school graduation, together, smiling.

The thing was, Sydney hadn't seen her mother since she was ten.

Sydney pulled the photo to her chest and cried like a baby.

15

Through her tears, Sydney found herself smiling at the photographs, even as an intense sadness cascaded over her. Merry had missed so many important events in her daughter's life, but she'd taken the time to secretly follow her progress. Why?

What would compel a mother to be a living ghost to her child's life?

The answers were inside these walls, she realized. Just as these pictures had been. With shaking fingers, Syd caressed the glass over her mother's face.

What a beautiful woman she'd been.

I do look like her.

She caressed the ringlets of her mother's hair and couldn't remember why she didn't ever let her hair stay curly instead of perming the natural wave into angel hair straightness.

Habit, nothing more. Sydney pulled the thin band from around her shoulder-length hair and let it fall.

Gusty wind shook the glass panes, and Syd realized she was still in the same spot where she'd stopped when she'd entered. Time had seeped by unnoticed, the same way morning slipped easily into afternoon.

She gently placed the photograph back onto the table and picked up the flashlight.

What other surprises awaited her?

Her heartbeat racing, she directed the light around the room and let the thrill of awe encompass her.

The dining and living rooms were not only lush, but they were feminine and tasteful. In the dark she could still make out the comforting pink and white furniture and accessories.

Around the room were a love seat, chaise longue and reclining chairs made for two in sturdy but feminine white leather and suede. The tables and entertainment center were made of white wood with glass doors and shelves. Everything in the room had soft edges for comfort and relaxation.

Sydney stepped farther into the room and realized her feet had sunk into the thickest carpet she'd ever touched. She kicked off her shoes and took another tentative step from the door and relished it.

This was heaven on earth.

Retracing her steps, Syd glanced into the kitchen, pleased that it was functional for the small size.

She held the flashlight in front of her as she walked down the small hallway and stood outside the closed door. This was Merry's bedroom. A place that was every woman's sanctuary. Sydney didn't know what to expect, but was suddenly more curious than afraid.

She pushed down the handle and entered paradise.

The bedroom was exquisitely decorated with the bed being the focal point. Built on a platform and surrounded by lace curtains, the king-size bed dominated the space, letting all who entered know this room was made for pleasure.

Sydney tried the wall switch, but the lights remained off.

Undeterred, she eased around the room, touching each surface of the beautifully crafted dresser to the blanket warmer, to the contraption of leather bands that hung from the ceiling.

Unsure what it was, she let her speculation simmer as she continued into the bathroom.

Sydney sighed, long and heavy.

The bathroom was a woman's dream.

A sunken tub that was at least seven feet long and about as wide, was the center of the room. Jacuzzi jets dotted the base and walls, and a tingle of naughty indulgence shot through Sydney.

For a woman Sydney hardly knew, she recognized that Merry's life had been about achieving the greatest and most carnal pleasures, but with class beyond anything Sydney had ever experienced in her life.

As she backed out she noticed a door and opened it to find a deep, narrow closet. Clothes were lined up by color and style, while shoes were lined on a shelf on the bottom row along the walls of the slender room.

Sydney ventured inside and inhaled deeply. Romance, by Ralph Lauren.

She couldn't keep her tears back. Romance was her favorite perfume also. She sank her nose into her mother's blouses and inhaled deeply.

The silk caressed her skin, the perfume linking them.

The flashlight dimmed a bit, and Sydney realized she'd have to be conservative with her limited resources. She searched the rows of clothes until she found crème satin pajamas and selected a pair that probably cost about half her weekly salary. Taking them with her, she left the closet, started the tub hoping enough hot water was left in the tank and went in search of another flashlight. In the living room, she noticed waist-high pillar candles. She wrestled one up on the bathroom counter and lit it.

The room was suddenly flushed with golden light.

Taking in the wall mirror opposite the tub, Sydney undressed, self-conscious.

A part of her anticipated someone walking in, demanding to know why she was there; yet another part was filled with wonder.

While Merry had been alive, mostly Sydney had dreaded meeting her, but now she was getting to know her mother better than if she'd been there in the flesh. Merry had left her a legacy. Her voice, though silent, still resonated.

The lukewarm water hugged Syd's skin and relaxed her. These were the pleasures her mother had enjoyed daily, the life Sydney so greatly desired. She closed her eyes and imagined a day of Merry's life and had to admit here she felt like a real woman.

Another minute passed before she opened her tired eyes and pulled her languid body from the water.

Outside, the wind and rain engaged in a jealous battle for dominance, each growing more aggressive as the night wore on.

Sleep was calling her, and Sydney wanted to answer.

Dressing in the pajamas, she gathered her clothes, unsure what to do with her laundry. She still wasn't used to this being her place, and she peeked around the corner before entering the bedroom, leaving the clothes on the dresser corner.

The temperature in the room had dropped, and she scurried around with the flashlight, searching for the thermostat. She found it and was shocked to see that it was a brisk forty-five degrees inside. It felt colder. Pushing the up lever a couple times, she waited to hear if it would click on, then realized it wouldn't work. The electricity wasn't on.

Back in the living room, she wondered what had become of Merry's life? Had she fallen in love again? Desired another man? More children?

Had she been happy?

At the entertainment center she found photo albums in rows by year. Sydney pulled the first one off the shelf and then headed into the closet for a sweater.

Merry had obviously been a woman of selective taste.

There was no thick cotton sweater, but instead lush and expensive cashmere.

Sydney slipped on the luxurious garment, then spotted a cabinet at the back wall. She pulled on the knob and gasped at the volumes of diaries. Pulling out the oldest one, she closed the door. The photo albums and this one volume were enough for tonight. Syd gathered everything, when her cell phone began to ring.

Curling up on the love seat, Sydney pulled the phone from her purse. "Hello?"

She'd hoped it would be Drew so she could sound cavalier and in control.

"How are you?"

"Hey, 'Vette, I'm good. I'm in Merry's apartment. Did you lose power?"

"Yeah, but what does it matter? I don't have a freezer full of food. I eat out almost every night. I'm just bored out of my skull. I saw the news. Tell me again, how'd you get away from the mob?"

Sydney didn't really want to explain. "I had help from a new friend."

"Male or female?" Evette asked, suspicious.

"Female. She was a cop, for goodness sakes. Why?"

"I'm just looking out for you. Earlier you were having dinner with the enemy. How'd it go?"

Strange, since I kissed him and nearly ended up in his bed. "Fine. Everything is just fine."

"Syd, you're keeping secrets, and if you don't want to be for real, then tell me to mind my own business. But don't give me that placid fine, just fine, as if this is an Oprah Winfrey interview."

Sydney sat on the love seat and leaned back, wishing she had a blanket. "Look, I'm sorry. I don't know what to say. Dinner was nice. He apologized, 'Vette. He seemed genuinely sorry."

"And you forgave him."

"Yes. Does that make me a traitor to my own self?"

"No, it makes you a vulnerable woman."

Sydney frowned. A year ago she'd had jury duty, and Dara Jones had been charged with the federal crime of aiding in a bank robbery because she'd driven the get-away car. At the trial she'd claimed she'd wanted to just talk to Denny Moore, the man who'd loved and left her. He'd promised to talk if she gave him a ride to the bank. She'd waited patiently for him until she'd been pulled from her car by the automatic-weapon-carrying SWAT team.

Despite her attorney's best efforts, the boutique owner had been sent to prison.

"You're quiet. What are you thinking about?" Evette asked.

"Dara Jones. She wanted answers about her relation-ship failure, and she's in prison for twelve years."

"Sydney Morris, have you done something stupid? I don't care what the TV says; I'm coming to get you."

Sydney chuckled, then yawned. "Don't get arrested. I'm not going to bail you out."

"You got jokes, but you didn't answer the question. Have you done something stupid?"

How could she tell her best friend she'd let Drew, her sworn archenemy, kiss her? "I wouldn't say it was stupid, and in my defense, I'd had too much wine."

"What the hell went on?"

"He kissed me. I mean, I kissed him. We kissed."

Silence grew long and lengthy until Syd couldn't stand it anymore. "Say something."

"In a way I'm relieved."

Sydney rubbed the crinkle between her eyes with her fingers. "What's that mean?"

"You haven't been interested in anyone in so long,

it's kind of a relief. But I'm worried that the first man that comes along, especially a man with whom you are embroiled in a lawsuit, you kiss."

Sydney sat up in the darkness. "I do sound vulnerable."

"That's all I'm saying, sweetie. But if you, Sydney, the most levelheaded, practical, pragmatic woman in Atlanta, tell me you know what you're doing, then I'll tell you to French kiss your heart out and use a condom. Don't answer! Let's save something for tomorrow. This storm isn't going away for another two days. Before we hang up I wanted to ask you, how is the place?"

Syd remembered her anger toward her mother and her resistance to this place. Now her feelings were not the same. "It's nice, 'Vette. Classy and elegant. I'm glad."

"Why?" Surprise showed in Evette's voice.

"I'm glad she didn't live in squalor. I'm getting to know her a little bit at a time, and that would have hurt me more. She died alone, and I wish she hadn't. I'm glad she had a decent quality of life."

"Syd, you never stop surprising me." Evette cleared the emotion from her throat. "Call me tomorrow. I'll try my best to get over there, okay?"

"Hey, thanks for not beating me up."

"Honey, that's what magazine articles are for. Go to bed."

"Bye."

Syd hung up the phone and reached for the charger before remembering she wasn't at her home.

Evette's words resonated. Sydney had to keep her head, or she could lose more than her store. She could lose her heart.

She hugged herself and stood, before going into the bedroom where she stopped at the door.

She couldn't sleep in Merry's bed. Entering the apartment, bathing in her tub and wearing her pajamas had been big enough firsts for one day.

Parting the curtain, she pulled off the thick comforter and took it to the living room to the recliner.

Syd snuggled in and sighed, wishing the heat worked. People would freeze to death tonight, and the thought saddened her.

I don't want to die alone, like my mother.

Her eyes drifted closed as sleep slipped over her like a romantic fragrance.

I won't. Drew is right next door.

Syd covered her face with the blanket and fell asleep.

16

The next morning, Drew heard Sydney moving around in her apartment, cabinets opening and closing, the tub running and then the front door slamming shut. She walked past his door and down the stairs without breaking stride, and he wondered where she was going.

He wanted to go after her, but discipline kept him in his seat, reviewing the schedule for the first week.

Half the night he'd lain awake listening for Sydney, wondering how she'd done her first night in a home she'd never known. Drew couldn't imagine not knowing his mother. He loved her deeply.

Roseanne Macbeth Crawford had been the backbone of the family, the strength he'd relied upon on those rare occasions when grief defied understanding.

To this day only select family members knew the full scope of his work with the bureau, and his mother knew only because he'd stumbled upon her past while working an old case. Life never ceased to amaze him.

Like now. He couldn't stop thinking about Sydney. Couldn't stop wanting her. The idea of being alone with her was so appealing, he got up and headed straight to the bathroom for a brutally cold shower.

If the heat didn't come back on soon, they were going to have some serious problems tonight.

Dressed in his warmest clothes, he listened as his phone buzzed against the butcher-block table. He grabbed it, standing to stretch.

"Hello?" he said, his breath blowing out in a fine mist.

"It's me, Mike."

"What's up?"

"I just completed a call from Horace from the city council. He basically echoed Julian. Sydney is the rightful owner of FLIRT. It doesn't matter that the property changed hands from mother to daughter. The property was willed to her."

"In a trust with conditions," Drew asked.

"Exactly. Our argument will be that an adult store must only be owned by a single person. A store in trust violates that ordinance, and since she has to meet the conditions of the will, she can't very well abide by both rules."

"Good." Drew sighed in relief. "What's the plan after that?"

"The church folks are going to turn up the heat."

"I'm not worried about them. I just want to make sure that we attack this from a legal standpoint," Drew stressed. "We are not behind nor do we support any personal attacks on Sydney."

"I agree. She's probably a nice lady, but stopping her from opening is our only goal. Thing is, Drew, you have to be in this for the long haul. Did you see the crowd outside her house?"

"I saw them. I hope we didn't have anything to do with that."

"We didn't, but as you can see, this has taken on a life of its own. I saw some footage taken at her house by a camera crew that had been attempting to set up from a neighbor's property. Their signal was mysteriously jammed, and I never got a clear picture of the cop's face, but there was something familiar about her. Know anything about two women sneaking out the back?"

Drew didn't blink. "Not a thing."

"Good." Mike didn't believe him, Drew could tell, but he didn't have facts, and he wouldn't make accusations without irrefutable evidence. "I'm damn glad to hear that. On last night's news they showed Sydney leaving her place under escort several hours after the two mystery women. Had a big suitcase with her. I wonder where she is now?"

Drew continued his game of mental semantics. "Can't help you there either."

"Well," Michael sighed, giving up. "I'd better go. The girls are making muffins."

"You have heat and electricity?"

"Definitely," Mike said smugly. "I'll check on you in a few days. Don't do anything you'll regret."

"Never." Drew shuddered in the cold, wishing he already hadn't.

He tried to work for an hour, but the colder it got,

the more he remembered the warmth of Sydney's mouth against his.

He worried about the heating situation, knowing they wouldn't make it another night without some source of heat. There was wood outside. He wasn't sure how much, but if worse came to worst, he might have to convince Sydney that sleeping with him could save both their lives.

Drew put on his coat and headed outside.

17

Sydney felt herself getting sleepy as she stood back in the fading daylight to examine the wall she'd just finished merchandising. The lingerie looked great.

She had corsets and bustiers, negligees and crotchless and bottomless leather chaps. Bras in red and pink to enhance small nipples and black and purple bras that had no nipples at all. On this wall was something for everyone from size zero to 4X.

Sydney tried to jog in place, but her cold feet refused to cooperate. Her breath puffed out, and she wondered if she was going to make it alone another night.

Last night she'd been cold, but today the temperature outside had dropped to an all-time low of minus-thirty degrees.

Atlanta was in the midst of the second worst ice storm in history.

She staggered as she loaded six- and seven-inch platform shoes on two mock staircases on either side of the lingerie wall.

She'd worked all day and into the evening transforming the store into a place women would love. But now she felt weak and numb. Maybe if she rested, her strength would return. Planning to go back to Merry's apartment, she transferred her toys and gels into a bag. Tonight she was going to have some fun all by herself.

Dizzy, Sydney held her head a moment and whimpered as she sank down on the bottom step. She'd dressed as warm as she could, wearing four sweaters over a pair of sweatpants with two pairs of stockings underneath. She'd even gone so far as to fashion a lovely tangerine colored cashmere sweater into a hat, but now she was light-headed and cold, and it was dark.

She had no choice. She had to find Drew.

Pushing to her stiff feet, Sydney gathered eight packs of batteries and the bag of sex toys and stumbled to the back door of FLIRT, more woozy than she'd realized.

She didn't want to go outside. What if she couldn't make it up the stairs to the apartment? What if she slipped on the ice and hurt herself? Who would hear her call for help?

This was hopeless. She'd pushed herself too far, and now she was in trouble. Sydney reassured herself that if she got upstairs and under the warm blankets, she'd feel better in the morning.

She just needed a minute to rest. Just a minute . . .

Her legs gave out, and she lay on the floor, cold wind whistling under the back door. She turned her face away and closed her eyes.

Maybe if she slept a little, her body would recover . . .

Her cell phone rang, and Syd talked to her grandmother. Madea often visited while Syd slept. She'd been in heaven for ten years.

Syd told her about her mother's apartment and how nice it was. And how she'd misjudged the woman whom she'd known only for a short time. She asked if Madea had seen Merry, but she just smiled, expressing her love.

Thunder filled the sky, shaking the air around Sydney. Madea kept talking, but Syd couldn't hear her.

Heavy thumps echoed; then cold air swirled. She called out to Madea but could no longer see her.

Suddenly she was floating, and excitement passed through Sydney. She was going to be with Madea again and maybe see her mother.

Drew's voice coaxed Sydney awake.

She couldn't understand why his voice was so near. She tried to move, but felt paralyzed.

A tear escaped her eye and slid down her cheek.

"Baby, open your eyes."

With great effort, she finally succeeded. Drew loomed over her, concern and fear etched deeply in his forehead.

"Where am I?"

"You're in the restaurant with me."

Tenderly, he brushed the hair from her forehead.

Sydney couldn't help it, but she was afraid. She shouldn't be here with him. Especially not burning hot as she was with Drew so close. "Why am I here?"

"You were trying to freeze to death in your store."

"I wasn't." She closed her eyes, remembering that

she'd been working in FLIRT, but had collapsed as she'd left. He'd obviously saved her life. She owed him thanks for that, but how could she be gracious under the circumstances? "You saved me?"

He brought a straw to her lips, and Sydney watched his eyes as she drank. Concern blended with caring.

"I'm better," she said and tried to sit up, but her body protested, and her head felt as if a boot had been planted right on top. "Hey, stay put, lady. You're not going anywhere."

When she stopped resisting her body fell back into its resting state. This felt better than anything. She looked out the corner of her eye and saw the fireplace. "How'd you know where to find me?"

"I got a frantic call from your friend Evette. She said you were in your store talking to Madea, your father's mother. Evette said Madea's been dead for ten years."

He caressed her forehead, and Sydney closed her eyes, ashamed. "I can't believe she told you that. You and I are enemies."

"Remember, neutral territory?"

The man that loomed above her hadn't stopped stroking her face. He hadn't left her side or seemed to want to deceive her. He'd saved her life, and he'd asked for a truce twice.

Who was the real Drew? The man who wanted to beat her out of her inheritance or the man who'd just rescued her?

Syd tried hard to judge him, but her judgment was as foggy as her head. She had to fly blind and trust only what her eyes could see. "Okay. Truce."

A pile of blankets was stacked on top of her. Then he looked above her head. Drew had fashioned some kind of tent out of blankets that held in the heat. "Did the heat come back on?"

"I wish," he said, tucking the covers around her more tightly. "I made a little cocoon for us in front of the fireplace. There's enough wood to last us for a while. You're lying on blankets surrounded by tables that are on their sides to insulate us as much as possible. I raided your apartment and mine for blankets to keep you warm. It's my fault that you're here. I don't know what I'd do if you got sick because of me."

Her gaze rested on the man who'd surprised her more than all the birthday presents she'd received in her life. Every time she thought she had Drew Crawford pegged, he took her to a new level.

"Am I sick?" she asked him, her eyes feeling heavy.

"Rest," he said softly. "I'm watching over you."

Sydney rocked under the weight of the blankets.

"Be still," he urged, his hands burrowing under the blankets to her arm. His fingertips caressed her skin, sending goose bumps fleeing up to her shoulders. "I want to lie on my side."

"Okay," he said, lifting the covers enough for her to settle down, facing him.

"I'm so tired, Drew. Will you sleep with me?" she asked, hoping he understood she meant for him not to leave her alone.

She wanted to look at his eyes again and know more about the man who smelled so good. She wanted to ask how he was able to touch her skin through her sweaters, and if he had living grandparents. She wanted to thank him for rescuing her, but her brain was sending instructions for her to rest.

Mostly she wanted to know why a man like him wasn't married.

The questions streamed like the words on the screen at a silent movie, but her mind wouldn't work right. Her lips wouldn't cooperate.

Sydney burrowed closer, inhaling him, and when she was close enough, she stretched out her arm and met him.

She sighed when warmth floated across her arm, then fell into a deep, satisfying sleep.

18

Drew awoke to the even sound of Sydney's breathing, and he tempered his shock at being wrapped around her and under her covers.

How much worse could he make the situation? Make love to her? Get her pregnant?

He stuck his head out of the blankets and prayed the heat was back on.

Disappointment assailed him. He was a protector, had been for the past twenty years. How had he lost his professional perspective in this case?

Sydney wasn't a client.

He hadn't been hired to keep bad guys away from her.

He *was* the bad guy.

Disentangling himself from her took some time, but when he was finally apart from her, his heart thundered in a wicked tempo.

She'd be asleep for a while longer, the crushed chamomile tea and brandy making a good hot toddy.

What was his problem? Sydney was just a woman.

A woman he'd have to leave alone.

He stoked the fire and stretched, before checking on her again.

She lay peacefully on her side, her legs having drawn up during the night. His body remembered her spooning him, how it felt to be so totally surrounded by someone, and he'd slept on, resting in the fairy-tale world he'd created.

Drew grabbed the flashlight and inserted fresh batteries, then headed up to his apartment and stripped.

The water was going to be ice cold, if the pipes hadn't frozen. And he deserved the punishment he was about to inflict upon himself for forgetting the goal.

Drew turned on the water and stepped inside.

Teeth clenched against the icy needles, he scrubbed himself until he was drawn up in every way. He had no right to lust after Sydney. Had no right to sleep with her. He'd had no right bringing her here.

And now she was sick, and that was his fault, too.

Shutting off the water, he toweled off and dressed quickly. There was no getting around it; this was the worst storm in Atlanta's history, and he wished like crazy it was over.

Gathering a few towels, a face cloth and soap, Drew made it back down to the restaurant and wondered what he could put together for breakfast. The restaurant was wired for electricity, but he had a grill outside and one tank of propane.

Except it was so damned cold outside, he didn't

think it wise to even try cooking something for her. He'd have to make do over the open fireplace. He needed to be near Sydney in case she got delirious or worse.

In the kitchen, he filled pots with water and managed to get food boiling when he heard movement behind him.

Sydney was on her knees, her head out of the makeshift bedroom.

"Hey," he said gently. "Lie back down."

"I need a toothbrush and the bathroom."

Her voice sounded unsteady, but that could be because she hadn't used it in twenty-four hours.

"I'll get some supplies from your apartment—" But he stopped when she shook her head.

"None of that stuff is mine. Toothpaste, two washcloths and a towel should do it, but the bathroom?"

"Right." He snapped out of his trance and helped her up. He guided her to the ladies' room and walked her in, when she turned to look at him. "I can handle the rest. I promise not to fall in."

Embarrassed, Drew started away, then stopped. "Will you call me when you're done?"

"I promise," she said, the blanket he'd placed around her shoulders dragging the floor.

"I'll be right outside."

"Drew," she begged. "Go away. I need to pee."

Executing an about-face, he double-timed it out of the restroom and back to the pot of boiling water. He ran back to the bathroom and hooked the bag of soap, lotion and toothpaste along with the towels on the door. Then he quickly prepared pasta, soup and vegetables.

He'd poured two bowls, when he sensed her behind him.

Turning, he nearly dropped the pot of food.

Sydney looked fresh-faced and young. The stress lines from previous days were gone along with her anger.

"Are you hungry?" he asked.

"Cold and hungry, yes," she replied, her arms coming around her.

Drew set down the pot and rushed to her. "You can eat in here." He indicated their makeshift campground. "Then it'll be time to rest."

"I'm not tired," she said, yawning. "What's going on out there?"

"I found a weather radio in the office at FLIRT and got some batteries."

"You've been in my store?"

"I was saving your life," he teased, taking her arm and leading her back into their warm room.

She looked around at their haven and back at him. "I'll have to thank you for that later."

Without sarcasm or rancor, her words reached him, and he could feel her thanks.

"No need." Drew covered her shoulders and tucked blankets around her legs. Then he passed her a bowl of soup.

"What is this?"

"Kitchen soup."

The spoon stopped halfway to her mouth. "Come again?"

Her skin glistened, and even with only the assistance of cold water and soap, he found her scent alluring.

"Kitchen soup is something my father used to make when he had to feed us kids. Anything that wasn't nailed down went into a boiling pot. Only because I like you did I limit my selections to edible products."

Sydney eyed him suspiciously, and he sucked in an involuntary breath. If he wasn't careful, things would get out of hand.

"Your father used to put inedible things in your soup? I can't believe that."

"He was a prankster. But he let us believe all kinds of things." Drew found himself smiling.

"Is he still alive?"

"Very much so. He lives south of Atlanta."

"Do you have a mother?"

What a strange question. But from Sydney and her background, he understood how something that sounded so odd was normal from her.

Drew nodded, eating, and was glad when Sydney started. "She's sixty-seven years old. She stayed home until we were nearly grown, then became a professional volunteer."

"That's admirable. How long have they been married?"

"Forty-five years. My brothers and sister are throwing them a huge party on their anniversary in four weeks."

"What about you?"

"I'm catering, of course."

"No kitchen soup, right?"

He felt himself grinning. "Filet mignon, grilled salmon, lobster—all my parents' favorites."

"Sounds delicious. I recall you telling me you have a twelve-year-old sister. How'd that happen? I mean I know, but—"

"She's my sister's child. My parents adopted her."

"How many brothers and sisters do you have?"

"Four brothers and two sisters. My sister Cassidy is deceased."

"Oh. I'm sorry."

"Thank you. It was a long time ago."

Drew remembered his sister's smiling face and her infectious laugh. He'd never known anyone as funny as she was. But then she'd strayed into a life of crime and had gotten caught up. She'd disappeared twelve years ago, and her remains had been identified five years ago in the Nevada desert.

No one knew why she'd gone all the way out there, and no amount of investigating had uncovered any answers.

Drew had never told anyone about Cassidy.

He looked back at Sydney, who'd finished her soup and was attempting to stand.

"Do you want more?" He took the bowl from her hands.

"No, Drew," she said, bumping him with her arm. "I can do this, you know. I'm not helpless."

He put the bowls down and had her on her back before she knew what hit her.

"You're not?" he asked, unable to help himself.

"What?" She smiled and tried not to look at him. He tipped her chin.

"Helpless?"

"No," she whispered, and then her mouth met his in a searing kiss.

A log slipped on the fire, causing the flames to shoot up, just as Sydney wrapped her arms and legs around him.

Drew pushed himself up on his hands and toes, taking her with him.

Her tongue laved his, and she caressed his bottom lip with hers. "Damn!" Several beats passed before he could speak. "Sydney, we can't do this."

"We're going to." Her mouth stroked his. "Kiss me, Drew."

He wasn't crazy. Sydney was out of her mind. She had been sick. Unconscious when he'd found her, and now she wanted human contact now that she was feeling better. This was a man's dream, but he couldn't take advantage of her.

Wouldn't.

But he didn't know how long he'd be able to resist if he kept her body against his, her mouth seeking completion with his.

The full-body push-up with her attached to him began to hurt, and he lowered himself onto her and hardened. Her legs were still around his back, and she sighed. "Finally."

The word nearly undid him. It was as if she really wanted him.

Drew held her hips still with every intention of leaving their private, warm sanctuary. He looked into her eyes, noticed her hair splayed across the pillow, and her mouth open and waiting.

"You trying to get me in trouble?"

"With whom?" she asked innocently.

"You. You're going to feel different about this come tomorrow. You'll blame me, and I'll blame myself for taking advantage of a sick woman. Besides, we're still embroiled—"

"Shh." She whispered something in his ear, then stuck her tongue inside.

Drew lurched and drove his hips into hers. Her legs locked behind his back.

"This is Switzerland, remember? Make love to me."

Beneath him, Sydney's sexy smile just about caved him in. Making love to her would be so easy.

She wriggled, until her sweater was beneath her breasts and his shirt was up, too.

Finally skin met skin.

"You're playing with fire," he assured her.

"I certainly hope so. Let's make the best of it."

Syd rose up on her elbows and caught his chin with her teeth. She nipped at him, and as his control slipped, he wanted to strip just enough to plunge himself into her. He loved her confidence and the fact that she wasn't what he expected.

"No regrets?" he asked for the final time.

"None." She reached under his double layer of sweaters and let her delicate fingers skate across his nipples.

Yearning tightened his groin, and he wanted to roar his release, but he slowed and started peeling off her clothes one excruciating piece at a time.

Drew rolled so Sydney was on top. She sat astride him, her shirt slipping down her perfect stomach.

Women with super athletic bodies had never interested him. He'd always gone for curvaceous, shapely women who possessed innate sex appeal.

Sydney was that woman.

Her stomach was soft, her coloring a delicious caramel. He wondered if she was as delicious as she looked.

Normally he'd take time on the back end of passion to admire a woman's skin color, but in the firelight, she looked like Aphrodite, the goddess of love sent to please only him.

Sydney pulled a long-sleeve T-shirt over her head, leaving her chest almost bare.

Drew ran his hands up her arms, and goose bumps skittered across her skin.

"Cold, baby?" he asked, feeling a brief flash of conscience.

"You'll warm me up." She reached around and unsnapped her bra, then held the front to her chest with her fingertips. The strap slid down her arm, and she looked at it, then gave him the sexiest come-and-get-it look he'd ever seen.

Drew sat up and claimed her breast.

"Yes, yes, yes," Sydney moaned so husky, he cupped and laved the other just to hear her say it again.

He parted with her for a second, removed his shirts and pants, then stripped her naked.

"God, you're beautiful." Her body awed him, the rise and fall of her chest letting him know this was real. He was making love to Sydney. He claimed her breasts again, desire escalating when her nipples bloomed against his tongue.

She writhed beneath him, breathing hard, her hands playing dangerous games across his back and chest.

He dipped his fingers into her folds, and she gasped, her legs shuddering beside his.

Drew waited patiently, looking down at her. Her eyes opened, and he felt himself slip into unchartered territory. The part of him that wanted to finish what he started didn't care. He wanted to witness the passionate release of Sydney Morris. "Open for me."

Her left knee slowly went up. She was letting him in, but it was at a great cost to her. Her eyes demanded release.

Drew obliged, kissing her from the soles of her feet, ending at her mouth, his fingers never leaving her nest.

She writhed and moaned, and still he held back from claiming her completely.

She clutched at his arms. "Lie with me."

"Come first."

There was no rhyme or reason to his desire to see her climax, yet he had to finish what he started. At the last second, his thumb flicked across her clit, and as her body arched, his tongue slid across her budded tip.

"Drew!" Sydney squealed in a melody so sweet, he knew this was all that he wanted.

19

Sydney didn't know what had happened to her. One minute she was on her back and Drew was making delicious love to her, and the next she was straddling his waist, their groins locked, their mouths melded.

She wanted him.

Especially after he'd made her body sing.

This wonderful glory wouldn't last, she knew. The exhilarating fantasy they were living out would screech back to reality with the return of the electricity, but for now in this restaurant, in the safety of his arms, this was all they had.

Sydney sat astride him, wanting him to experience the same level of pleasure he'd given her.

Logs on the fire slipped and flashed, the firelight dancing against the walls of their crude little cove. But he'd saved her from death, and now was infusing a level of existence into her body that she'd never known.

"It's so good," she moaned. "So much better than I ever imagined," she confessed, pleased that he brought protection and had already brought her to a shattering climax.

"I promised you my 'business' would be."

The sexiest bubble of laughter shook her chest. "You were right."

A day's growth of hair covered his jaw, his mouth slack, his lips moist. She scooted closer and clenched, breaking his rhythm. His gaze shot to her, and he gave her the sexiest smile.

"Ready?" she asked him, wrapping her arms around his neck. She played with his back and neck, nuzzling his collarbone.

His hands cupped her bottom, and he pushed in and held her there.

"Damn ready."

Another trip to bliss began, and Sydney squeezed her eyes closed. His mouth tortured her, and her breathing came in short staggered bursts.

"Not again," she moaned, although the words weren't a complaint.

"No?" he asked, slowing, his beard blazing a path of desire down her chest to her nipples. Need rushed from both ends of her body and met between her legs.

"Not alone," she managed, her hands on his shoulders.

Sydney's heart quickened, and her hips followed the pace set by his hands.

Her head fell back, and he caught the tip of her nipple between his lips and drew in softly.

Sydney felt as if her body would burst. She rushed

him, staving off the inevitable, until she couldn't fight the wicked sensation any longer.

She caught his face between her hands and stared him in the eye, whispering, "Come with me."

She tightened, her body gripping him, and he tensed. For one second they were frozen, and then they exploded.

20

Sydney purred when she slept, like a contented kitten.

As Drew lay awake, he wondered how much more he could screw up his life and that of the woman beside him?

He'd wanted to make love to her, had to answer that animalistic need inside himself to claim her, but even as she slept in her innocence, she'd stolen something from him.

Disentangling his limbs from hers, he covered the body he'd ravaged with layers of blankets as if that would somehow prevent him from returning for more.

The fire had died down, the cold air encasing him in the hard reality.

He'd screwed up big-time.

Pulling on his clothes and boots, he decided to forgo his jacket and went outside for firewood. Sparkling white snow covered every surface, but the bitter wind had quieted, letting him know that the storm would soon be at its end.

Still, winter punished his bare skin, clawing at him as he set about the chore of gathering wood.

Cold against his hands, he didn't stop stacking until he couldn't see above the logs.

Fighting with the temperature and the weight of the wood, he staggered but gained his footing. He deserved the punishment.

Deserved to feel the biting pain as the bitter air seared his lungs. Maybe now he'd regain his perspective.

He'd been a maintenance man, and what he was feeling was deeper than his usual after casual sexual feelings.

Generally, he did his homework upfront, and he and his women had an understanding.

It was sex and sex only.

That was somewhat the case now with Sydney.

After today, they'd go back to fighting for what each wanted. Adversaries once again.

Drew managed to get inside and drop the wood inside the hallway, taking only a few of the drier logs to the fireplace.

How could he keep fighting now that he and Sydney had become lovers?

Because he was mortgaged, leveraged and in hock up to his neck. Satisfaction had to succeed.

That meant FLIRT had to fail.

Despite what Mike had said, there was no learning to live together.

The only solution Drew could think of was to buy her out, but with what?

With a pot of warm water from the fireplace, he washed himself and changed, then headed back to the restaurant fireplace and started water boiling and the food they'd have for the day.

The weather would break today. It had to.

Sydney hadn't stirred yet, and he didn't want to be close when she did. Seeing her would make him want her.

He turned to leave when bells started ringing from timers and appliances in the kitchen. The lights flickered on, and voices from the TV filled the room.

Hopefully the heat would soon follow. And life would return to normal.

Drew sensed Syd awake behind him.

He turned, and all the resolve he'd claimed while outside in the snow melted.

"Morning," she said, groggy.

"Morning, darlin'." Inwardly, he cringed at the intimate pet name, but he couldn't take the word back.

"It's still cold."

He nodded, his gaze returning to the fire and the bubbling pots.

"Something smells good. More kitchen soup?"

He grinned, but didn't look back at her. "Nope. The breakfast of champions, or the best we can do under the circumstances. Salmon, beans and rice."

"Sounds like a feast to me."

Syd touched him, and he turned automatically.

The movement had been involuntary as she stretched like a cat, her back arched off the floor, the thick layers of blankets slipping off her right breast.

Her nipple bloomed in the cold air as it had against

169

his tongue, and his mouth watered, his dick jumping ready to play.

Syd slowly looked at him and smiled.

He released the handle on the pot he'd been grip ping, but only to grab the handle of another. "I made some hot water for you whenever you're ready to bathe."

She wiped her eyes. The gesture made her look swee and innocent. "I'm ready now, and then we should talk about where we go from here."

"I was thinking the same thing."

Drew carried the pots of water to the bathroom and filled the sink. The amount looked paltry, but hot wate was a luxury. One he was sure Sydney would be grateful for.

He left her to her own devices and completed thei food. By the time she'd gone to her apartment and dressed, he felt strong enough to behave like a reason able man.

The newscasters confirmed that the city had been paralyzed by ice and snow.

EMTs, police, fire and rescue squads had been dis patched to handle emergency calls only and would hope fully get to every call before the night was over.

Sydney walked around the corner, and his tongu stuck to the roof of his mouth.

She'd pulled her hair up on her head and was wear ing a white turtleneck sweater and a red plaid shirt ove tight jeans. She looked good, even in her mother' clothes.

"Any good news?" she asked.

"The storm has stalled, and better weather is on th

ay tomorrow. Emergency personnel are trying to get
o every call. Here, eat."

They ate in silence, watching the news. He wanted to
t with her and eat as if it were any ordinary day, but he
te quickly and busied himself making sure the freezers
ere operational and the rest of the radios had fresh
atteries.

After watching the heroic efforts of the rescue crews
n TV, he felt as if he should be helping, but he couldn't
ave Sydney alone. He'd never forgive himself if some-
ning else happened to her.

He walked back into the dining room, and she was
anding by the booth, running her hands up and down
er arms. "Cover up before you have a relapse."

Sydney climbed in the booth where he'd put several
lankets and covered herself. "Drew, you can stop tak-
ng care of me. I'm fine. A little warm, in fact. Feverish,
think."

He was on her in an instant, his hand on her fore-
ead.

Inches apart, she looked up at him. "I was wondering
you were going to kiss me hello."

"That isn't a good idea."

Her eyes took on a serious glow. "We'll be enemies
omorrow. The weather will break, and you'll go back to
rying to open up a stuffy restaurant, and I'm going to
o next door and sell sex toys." Her breath caressed his
heek.

"You've changed."

"I hope so. Being kidnapped does that, you know."

Drew dragged his thumb across her lips. "But I saved
our life. That makes me the good guy."

Sydney licked his finger. "You saw me naked."

"You stripped me naked," he shot back.

"You kissed my feet."

"You liked it."

Their lips met, and he tried to put his internal war aside.

"But this isn't right. Tomorrow—"

"Will be here soon enough." Sydney's phone buzzed and he was grateful.

She reluctantly took it from her pocket and cut it off, setting it on the table. "I'd like to watch TV."

Drew palmed the remote and looked up at the mounted screens all around the room. But only the two televisions nearest the fireplace were working.

Sydney slid off the bench and started away, snagging his hand as she went. "In bed."

She led him to their crude bedroom, and at that moment, he realized he'd have followed her anywhere. He muted the TVs and slid the remote on a table as they passed.

Pulling Sydney by the pocket of her jeans, he cradled her in his arm, and when she was almost close enough he brought her against him. "You think you're running things, don't you?" he whispered.

Her eyes gave away her intense desire. "Someone had to be in control. You were taking too long."

As she talked he stripped her down to the skin and then followed her inside their haven. Sydney smelled of soap and perfume.

She looked like beauty and lust.

He kissed her all over, making her laugh as he tongued

her toes. She cooed when he nipped her hip and cried when he sank his fingers and tongue into her.

But Sydney was nothing if not full of surprises.

She shocked him when she mouthed the condom and sheathed him like a pro, and he was only too glad to sink himself into her.

Drew thought he'd take her on a quick ride to fulfillment, but as he moved inside of her, his body and mind urged him to savor every second.

He slowed, and she stayed in sync with his rhythm. Her golden eyes focused on his, and her gaze reached into his soul and shook loose the barrier he'd encased his heart in. Unlike any other time in his life, Drew felt out of control.

His blood heated, and his pace quickened. As much as he loved making love, Sydney was invading private places no one had ever been before. He had to finish and never touch her again. He wished he could walk away now, but they were too far gone to turn back. He closed his eyes against the lure of hers, but she reached up and captured his face in her hands, and like a magnet and metal, their mouths connected.

Drew pushed into her hard, and she accepted the power of each thrust with a slight hitch of her breath. He was accustomed to women climbing the walls, climaxing until their bodies gave out in exhaustion, but Sydney met him stroke for stroke, and he felt himself rushing to an end he normally savored alone.

He couldn't let himself come first.

That was the first rule in the maintenance man rule book.

If everybody got theirs in the right order, then there

was no need for pillow talk, lengthy goodbyes or false promises.

"Come, Sydney," he coaxed, watching her skin glowing.

She took in four quick breaths, and Drew made the mistake of looking into her eyes.

Suddenly her nether walls gripped him, and he knew he was lost.

"After you," she said.

Drew strained, grit his teeth and felt the burn of the fireworks he created.

21

Drew lay spent above her while Sydney accepted his crushing weight. She loved the feel of him and savored it, knowing this would be the last time. Her heartbeat skipped at the thought. She'd come to enjoy the feel and smell of him. The texture of his skin against her tongue, the way his voice sounded to her ears.

She'd once heard it took a person seven times before something was emblazoned in their memory. Syd was sure that was wrong. She'd made love to Drew three times, and each time a memory had been added to her brain. In lazy circles, she caressed his back.

"Tell me about your life," she asked, and he told her, sharing desires and goals that had made him into the man he was today. She wanted the long version, and when he'd reached the reason why she was in his arms, he made love to her again.

He made her call his "business" something she'd never said before, then rewarded her with a blazing orgasm that had created its own heat.

They slept, then awakened, talking more until she felt as if she'd known him her whole life.

Later they watched the fire in silence.

Pounding against the restaurant door made them jump apart. She looked at her bare self, and then at Drew. He looked as calm as ever. Unfazed by the fact that he had indeed screwed her brains out.

"People," she breathed, searching for her underwear. Her hands moved frantically through the plush mattress of blankets for her clothes. "Go get the door."

"Sydney, we need to talk."

She dressed hurriedly on her knees, forgetting the cold. "Drew, hurry. Never mind. I'll get it. They might be hurt and need help."

Her words seemed to spur him into action. He threw on jeans and his sweatshirt.

Sydney beat him to the door and turned the top lock.

"Wait, it might be reporters," Drew hissed so close to her ear fear skittered down her spine.

What he said was true, but she had the feeling if she stayed with him another night, she'd forget the point of owning FLIRT and give away all she was fighting for. She had to get out while she could.

"I'm not scared of them anymore."

Syd pulled the door open.

Evette leapt into her arms as they were surrounded by some of Georgia's finest firemen.

"You're alive. I was so worried."

Syd hugged her friend back. "How'd you manage to get the fire department to come with you?"

"When we last talked, you were incoherent. I was afraid you were dying. I called them, but they couldn't get out either. I tried everyone I knew and finally got the number to this restaurant. I asked Drew to check on you."

Sydney looked over her shoulder at the man she'd just let ravish her body and was embarrassed, even if no one knew what had happened, except them.

"Thank you for coming for me," she said to Evette, looking at Drew.

His eyebrow arched at the double entendre, but Sydney turned her attention to the unexpected rescue squad. "Can you take me home?"

Drew went into the kitchen, leaving her alone for the first time in days.

"The roads are still pretty bad, ma'am," the captain stated, his blue-eyed gaze slightly curious. "Only emergency vehicles are allowed on the road. Your friend took a serious chance getting here. But, we can call for a police escort. It may take a few hours. They're busy trying to clear the roads of stranded vehicles and answer serious emergencies. Do you need medical assistance?"

Sydney felt like a chastened child as she guided them the long way around the makeshift bedroom, to the booth where she'd shared her meals with Drew. "I was well taken care of."

The firemen took in the crude bedroom and traded knowing glances. The captain spoke quietly to several of the firemen, and they headed toward the door.

Sydney couldn't even look at the blankets and their

disheveled state. They told too many stories. "We were freezing to death. This is the only room with a working fireplace. We've been here nearly three days in the cold and in the dark."

She spoke defensively, but let the anger go. Had she walked in on this situation, she'd have made the same assumption.

"You fared better than some," the captain said. "We've already recorded seventeen deaths."

Drew walked back over to the fireplace for the pot of water. "Captain, I have some coffee, if you and your men are interested. It's not as good as it could be, but—"

The captain smiled. "That's the best offer we've had all day."

The men trooped into the kitchen, leaving Sydney and Evette alone in the booth.

"You slept with him," Evette said.

"Yes, I did." Syd met her friend's gaze and didn't feel an ounce of regret or sadness. What she'd shared with Drew was a lusty tryst under extreme circumstances that would never be repeated.

"You liked it!" Evette's look of awe struck a chord with Sydney. She couldn't hide her smile.

"Yes, I did."

"Well, fine. Somebody is going to get hurt. I can feel it. But one, that's none of my business, and two, it will probably be me."

"What are you talking about?" Sydney could still feel Drew's touch on her skin.

"How do you think I got here?"

"You rode in the fire truck?"

"No! I'm not trying to get him fired."

"Who?"

"The captain," she said softly.

"What's your connection to him?"

Evette looked toward the kitchen, lowering her voice, a sheepish smile on her face. "We're seeing each other. But no one knows." She sighed heavily. "I explained the situation and asked him to meet me here."

"You're not emergency personnel."

"I realize that."

"What aren't you saying, Evette? Is he married or something?"

Her friend's mouth pulled back into a line. "Separated. Papers signed, the hearing is next week."

Sydney looked at her friend long and hard. "What are you doing?"

Evette got up and huddled in her coat. "I'm freezing. You want coffee?"

"No," Syd said. "Answer my question."

"I like him a lot. Who knows if anything will develop, but I don't want to turn my back on the opportunity."

"Then go for it. Just be careful."

The men came out of the kitchen, to-go cups in hand. "We'd better get back to work. Ma'am," the captain said to Sydney, "I'm glad you're in good health." His gaze darted to Evette, and a heated look passed between them.

"Thank you for the rescue. I'm grateful for your help."

One of the firemen who'd stepped outside earlier rushed back in. "We've got a call, and the police were nearby and are outside if Ms. Morris is ready to return to her home."

Sydney looked at Drew. His face was a careful blank page, but she saw the question in his eyes.

What would she do?

Staying would mean she wanted to be there with him. Staying would mean their time together had validity. Staying would mean she'd lose FLIRT and her inheritance.

A war took place inside her, and she had never felt so torn apart by a decision.

Sydney walked toward Drew, and his eyebrows ratcheted up an inch. She picked up the jacket she'd been given by Asia and her two-women team. "I have to go."

With a last look, she slipped her arms into the sleeves.

"Five hundred thousand dollars."

Everyone looked at him in stunned silence.

Sydney knew he was offering her money for FLIRT, but as she'd come to realize, she now wanted more than money.

"Not your best." Sadness filled her heart. She couldn't have what she wanted.

Evette glanced between the two of them and held out both hands.

"Syd, you don't have to leave unless you want to. I thought you needed to be rescued."

"I do."

For the first time in three days, Drew was no longer the center of Sydney's world.

22

The ringing phone wore on Drew's nerves. He'd already answered it sixteen times, creating sixteen holes in the once packed reservation list.

He wasn't a man given to panicking, but he had to admit his nerves needed a good belt of Hennessey to settle down.

He walked back to the table where he'd been meeting with Mike and Julian and sat down. "We lost ten thousand dollars' worth of stock from the freezers. That's unrecoverable. If I start filing claims, I'll lose my insurance."

"Just order more. We can cover the losses."

"Replacing all that food is the problem. Every restaurant in three states is in the same position. I have a few connections, but not so many that I can replace all the meat I've lost."

"What can you get?"

"Fresh fish, a little beef, vegetables and appetizers."

His cousins' expressions mirrored how he felt inside. "I know doomed when I see it. Damn." Drew looked back at the inventory sheet, then shoved it away.

"Just calm down," Michael said dismissively.

"Calm down? Do you have an extra ten Gs lying around and three sides of beef, because I don't."

"Drew, we lost a little food. We can claim the loss on the taxes. And, we can come up with a viable plan B before the opening next week. Lori King and her client were informed today that the injunction has been lifted. FLIRT now has the crack in the door it needs to have its business license reinstated."

A delivery truck rumbled to a stop in front of FLIRT. From his seat, Drew could see the driver making trips inside with packages. Sydney supervised the delivery from start to finish, standing outside in a long sweater, jeans and boots. He wanted to tell her to put on her winter coat, the pink one, but he couldn't. They hadn't spoken in six days.

The nearly spring air whipped her hair, and she held it back with her hand, the other around her middle. She seemed to look right at him, their eyes meeting like shadows on a moonlit lake. He wanted to go to her, wrap his arms around her and nuzzle into her neck as he'd done when she'd been asleep.

She'd caressed his head in her slumber, her hand drifting over him, coming to rest on his back. And just as he remembered the displeasure of being trapped in Berlin under dubious circumstances, he remembered with mind-boggling clarity every nuance of her touch.

Drew wished his cousins weren't there. Then he could go outside and talk just to hear her voice.

The driver handed her the invoice, and she went back inside.

A connection had forged during those nights they'd been forced to be together. After he'd acknowledged that his attraction was real, he hadn't minded taking care of her. He could admit only to himself that his greatest pleasure was seeing Sydney when he woke up.

But that fantasy had ended courtesy of the fire department.

It was just as well.

Sydney represented the death of his dream. His restaurant would become another statistic if the doors to FLIRT were allowed to open.

"Julian, is there anything we can do?" Drew asked.

"Buy her out."

"I've already offered her half a million dollars."

"What!" his cousins exclaimed. Julian reared back on two legs on the chair.

"The will offers her three-quarters of a million. I can't beat that," Drew argued. "But I was trying to come close. I have property. I can sell off Lake Uniquoi."

"First, I'm not going to ask how you got that information regarding her mother's will. And second, that's family land," Julian ground out. "Selling it is out of the question."

"I can do what I damn well please!" Drew swore in German. He got up, angry with himself for blowing up. Michael and Julian watched him pace the floor, waiting for him to cool off.

"If she would have said yes, I would have sold the land to someone in the family. I don't want my restaurant to fail."

Neon pink lights flashed, and Julian and Michael followed the direction of Drew's gaze.

TOYS. ADULT MOVIES. FLIRT.

The words flashed hot pink and cast a shadow on the glistening mahogany tables in the restaurant. Sydney popped outside to look at the signs, and he got the distinct impression even she was surprised at their brightness.

No one could miss the smile on her face when she walked back inside.

Thick silence hung between them, and neither Julian nor Michael said a word when the letters started to blink and twinkle like Christmas lights. Finally they went off.

"You've got a problem," Julian announced.

"We can negotiate about the lights," Michael said quietly.

A car pulled down the drive and stopped in front of FLIRT. Two men got out, and one took pictures while the other hoisted a TV camera onto his shoulder. Great, that was exactly what FLIRT needed. More free publicity.

"I can understand your panic." Julian wiped his mouth. "I want to point out that selling the beach property won't accomplish your goals. Your shares are worth a lot less than a million dollars, and unless you want to liquidate all of your assets, which I wouldn't advise, you need a better plan. Have you considered moving Satisfaction?"

Drew shook his head. "I bought this place after it had been empty for three years. Unless it burns to the ground, I'm stuck here."

"I hope you don't mind me saying this, but you may have to keep her as a neighbor," Julian informed him.

The phone rang, and Drew made no move to answer it. "My customers will mind. We have a week. Do we go ahead with the radio ads? Those are the only ads that haven't been paid for. The newspaper announcements and invitations were all sent out weeks ago."

Michael, who'd been staring at his hands, looked at him. "You don't have a choice. You have to go through with it. In order for you to succeed, you have to act like you want this restaurant to be the best in town. Or you could delay the opening."

"What would that accomplish?"

"It could separate you from FLIRT. You won't be competing for parking space or the customers' attention. It'll give you time to think about what the best approach should be."

Drew considered everything his cousin had proposed. "All previous publicity efforts like the press releases and the announcements have the fourteenth on them. I can't not open now. Everything is on the line. I've got to make it work."

The phone rang again, and Julian picked it up.

"Satisfaction. Yes, we'd be glad to process your cancellation. February fourteenth? No problem." He covered the phone with his hand enough so the caller could still hear him. "Make a note to tell Lauren Michaels' assistant that she can have an extra table for her entourage. We had a premiere cancellation." He uncovered the phone. "Thank you for calling—oh, you'd like to keep your reservation? You'd like four more? I'm sorry, we don't have any availability."

Drew nodded quickly. They were down to ten tables booked; whereas before, all sixty had been taken, and they'd had a waiting list.

"We'll have to put you on the waiting list. Thank you, Paige. Please give Ms. Chastain our best."

Julian put the phone down and crossed his arms. "What?"

Drew couldn't believe that Julian, the straightest of all the Crawfords, had done something so . . . underhanded. "Lauren hasn't agreed to sing on the fourteenth."

"Then you'd better make sure she's here, because that's what I'm going to tell every caller from here on out. Also, my son is in a band. I might not like their music, but other Gen Xers do. Have you thought of inviting them down here for a guest appearance during the first week?"

Adrenaline pumped through Drew. "No. That wasn't the kind of restaurant I'd planned. Gen X people never entered my thoughts."

"That's a damned shame, especially since they have money and you're one of them."

Drew didn't walk around with his stomach showing and holes poked in his face. He wasn't emotionally deficient, and he didn't live with his mother. As far as he was concerned, he'd fallen into the hole between the baby boomers and the lost X generation.

But Julian made a valid point. He would talk to Chaz.

Using entertainment as a draw might get people to forget his neighbor sold sex toys.

"You have to pay them," Julian told him. "I can't wait for the day that boy gets a real job and moves into a real apartment."

Michael stood, patting his stomach. "I've got two sweet little girls at home. I got nothing to worry about."

Julian looked at Michael as though he was crazy. "You've obviously forgotten about Shayla's spoiled late teens and twenties until she married Jake. Tracy and Trina and the thirty-seven jobs they've had between them since they graduated college five years ago."

Drew grinned. "What about the boys finishing college with degrees and doing nothing meaningful with them. And Justin's boy taking off from Georgia Tech to travel the country with his wheelchair-bound girlfriend who wants to try her hand at being a travel writer?"

Julian and Drew laughed and slapped five.

"I may not have kids," Drew tossed out, "but I know that as soon as you and Terra complete the adoption process, those two sweet girls are going to turn into demons in Prada shoes. I saw seven-year-old Tif looking at the magazine the last time she was over to the house."

Mike looked like a deer caught trying to cross Jimmy Carter Boulevard at Interstate 85.

"Prada?" Mike choked. "I don't even buy Terra Prada. My girls aren't going to go crazy. They love me and their new momma."

Drew and Julian burst out laughing.

Julian balled up a sheet of paper and aimed at the

waste paper basket. "As sure as this is two points, they will nut up on you."

Michael tried to block the shot, but wasn't fast enough. The paper landed with elegance inside the can.

The challenge had been issued.

Tables were moved and chairs pushed aside. Normally family basketball games took place on the court at Uncle Julian's house, but it was still too cold out. This makeshift court would have to do.

Michael retrieved the ball of paper and reinforced it with another sheet.

"My girls are good and talented, and the little one is attached to me as if I were her own daddy. She's going to stay my baby forever." He aimed, and the shot was rejected by Julian, who couldn't catch his breath for laughing so hard. Mike tried to block him, but Julian easily lobbed the ball to Drew, who laid it in.

"She's going to be the one to break your heart," Julian promised him. "And you're going to wonder how you can still love her. But you will."

Drew pitched the ball to Mike, who shot from the makeshift free throw line.

"You're wrong. You'll see."

Drew smiled at his cousins, wishing he were as close to his siblings. They'd chosen different paths, and his years doing confidential government work hadn't played well when the truth had come out. They'd always had one impression of him, and it had been false.

Lies inevitably ruined everyone's life.

His cousins continued to shoot hoops, and he went

back to the table and reviewed his plan for the week. He would go through with the ads and check into the value of the lake property. If he needed to liquidate, he'd at least have some of the necessary information in place. And then he'd make Sydney his best and final offer.

At two in the morning, any normal person should be sleep, Drew thought, lying in bed, tossing from one side to the other. But he'd never been accused of being normal.

He was restless, and he craved the one thing he knew he couldn't have.

Flipping over, he reached for the remote and turned on the TV to distract himself from thinking about her. She was right next door. He'd heard her come in an hour ago. The tub had run, and finally she'd gotten into bed. He knew all of this because they shared a common bedroom wall.

Now that the heat was back on, he wondered if she remembered how sick she'd been. How he'd shared his body heat and so much more with her. He couldn't seem to forget.

Everything about her stayed with him. The scent of her perfume, the feel of her skin—like milk against his. Her taste and her golden eyes.

All his life people had commented on the color of his eyes. It was as if a black man with dark gray eyes was rare, but in his family that was the norm with all the men having one shade of gray or another.

Sydney had never said a word about his eyes. The

color hadn't mattered to her. She was either happy with him or angry, but she wasn't bowled over by "pretty eyes," and for many reasons, he liked that.

He hit the remote, changing the channels, and stopped, sitting up.

Sydney was on TV—again. "I don't have a grudge against my neighbor for starting this feud. I respect his right to his opinion, but FLIRT isn't going anywhere. We're inviting everyone, especially women, to come out and experience an adult store that caters to women. We have lingerie, aids for pleasure and many exciting additions that encourage women and men to put her needs first."

"How do you think Mr. Crawford will react to the change of heart of the city council?"

"I don't know, but he's a grown-up. We all have to deal with disappointment."

"Will you ever eat at Satisfaction?"

Sydney smiled. Her lips looked delicious. Drew wished he hadn't noticed. "I've already eaten there. The food is outstanding."

Drew sat up, shocked.

"You're kidding," the interviewer said, trying not to laugh. "He tried to put you out of business, and you ate at his restaurant?"

"Mr. Crawford and I have a relationship—of sorts. We've agreed to disagree. Besides, I couldn't pass up his salmon, the special stuffed mushrooms and the filet mignon. After you visit FLIRT, pop next door and have an appetizer."

Drew rose.

"Now you're pitching his restaurant? Unbelievable.

You do know that there are people who are coming out just to support Satisfaction?"

"I'm not surprised. I sincerely hope the restaurant does well."

"How well?"

"Drew and I may never be more than neighbors, but I want him to succeed. I hope he feels the same about me."

"Well, you heard it first from Sydney Morris, the official owner of FLIRT. Find the right toy for your needs and then pick up an appetizer at Satisfaction. This is Barry Applegate, reporting from Northeast Atlanta."

Drew lay back on the bed and pondered the definition of the word *screwed*.

Sydney was playing a serious mind game on the public. She wanted that inheritance money bad, and she was doing whatever it took to get it.

He had a good mind to go over there and claim what his body insisted was his.

She'd cheated in their lovemaking encounter the last time, but he was sure that wouldn't happen again. He was in control. The days they'd been apart had restored his faith in his ability to please a woman until *enough* was the only word she could utter.

A little yelp pierced the fog in his brain, and he muted the television. What was going on next door?

His skin had a mind of its own, remembering her touch as if she were caressing him now, recalling the sound of her voice raised in passion's call and the lyrical melody as she descended.

He was hard instantly, wanting her.

Drew didn't pace as he'd intended, but left his apartment for hers. He could have gotten in had he wanted to, but she had to invite him in.

He knocked, not even sure Sydney would answer. Obviously she could achieve pleasure without him. But he hoped what they had was more than just an encounter between two desperate people.

Drew knocked again.

"Who is it?"

Her voice washed over him like warm rain in summer. "Sydney, open the door."

"It's late," she said, breathless. "What do you want?"

"I want—" He couldn't stop his heart from racing, or the yearning to be hip-deep inside of her. He had to have her.

"You. I want you. Open—"

The locks slid back, and the knob turned. His dick jumped, and he pushed the door until he saw her.

Wrapped in a towel, she stepped back on one foot. Drew followed her inside.

"You shouldn't be answering the door dressed like that."

The towel slipped down her right, then left, side. "Would you prefer this?"

Drew had never seen anything so erotic, as the woman standing naked except for the swath of cotton at her feet. "Sweet."

She backed up. "I knew it was you."

He pulled his T-shirt over his head and followed her as she inched backward. "How?"

"You couldn't sleep," she said quietly. "Every time you turned over—"

His shorts were kicked off, leaving him as nude as her. "What?"

"Your bed would bump the wall. It got me—" Sydney blushed.

He backed her into the bedroom door. Her cheeks were visible by shimmering candlelight.

"What?" Drew nudged her feet apart, then wedged his leg between hers. He sank his fingers into her, and she inched up the door, gasping. Her nipples were like erasers on his skin. He was aware of every inch of her. How it felt to be inside her. Drew stroked her deftly and savored the feel of her wet heat. "Say it."

"Horny for you!"

Her words were like a thousand wet dreams rolled into one.

He felt like a champion racehorse, already a winner, yet proud to prove it again. But this time, he'd have Sydney on his terms.

Leaning into her, he dragged his mouth down her neck, while his fingers continued their magic between her delicate folds.

Her staggered breathing enticed him; the quick rise and fall of her chest against his made him lean in. He smelled her pleasure, and when he had her on the brink, he massaged her G-spot and sent her flying solo.

Before recovery brought reason into their nest, he carried her to bed, sheathed himself from one of the many condoms on the bed, then plunged into her until the backs of her thighs rested atop his.

Her mouth opened, and he claimed her lips. He pushed and she moaned; he breathed out and she in.

He wanted to take her to new heights, when a steady churning near his head interrupted his thoughts.

"What is that buzzing?"

"Nothing," she said, her hand fanning out beneath the pillows.

He suckled her nipples, until he felt her muscles contract around him. He was relentless in his pursuit of her pleasure, and he wasn't going to stop until he'd had his fill. He drove into her, pinning her hands beneath the pillows.

In this position, he had access to every delectable tip of her.

Drew took advantage, making her body shudder.

"The truth?" he asked her.

"They're vibrators. I was pretending they were you."

He knocked the pillow on the floor and saw a half dozen of them in all shapes and sizes.

Knowing what she'd been doing sent him deeper into her.

"Have mercy," she begged, twisting in his arms. "Drew, oh, goodness, wait," she begged, panting, "or I'll explode." She lifted her hips, but that only drove him deeper against her tender spot.

"That's the point, baby."

All this time he'd done everything to prolong their inevitable climax, but now he felt bliss crawling up the soles of his feet.

She was wide open to him when he pulled the oval-shaped egg from the top of the bed and pressed it against her clit. He whispered in her ear, "Sydney, come for me."

Her whole body wrapped around his, and she exploded like the Fourth of July at Stone Mountain Park.

Drew finally let himself go, knowing that the line between sin and pleasure had never been closer.

23

Sydney lay against Drew's back, her body cupped against his. Them being together wasn't supposed to happen, but since it had, she had to face reality. There was something indefinable between them.

She wanted to give herself room to gain some perspective, but emotionally she'd been here before, so maybe it was appropriate that her arm was pinned under his.

Ever since childhood, she'd avoided intense emotion, afraid that her feelings would continue to be ignored.

But here in this heavenly bed, in this romantic room with a man who made her body feel things she'd never thought possible, she wondered what would be the outcome if she opened that tiny door inside her heart.

Sydney sighed deeply, still a little scared.

She'd never been a chance taker. She'd never won a

race, but she never finished last. She'd never known the euphoric joy of a blazing victory, or the gut-wrenching pain of defeat. She'd never followed the song maker's suggestion and dreamed the impossible dream—and lived it.

And now, if it were at all possible, she wanted to at least meet the emotion that knocked on the door of her heart.

Sydney closed her eyes, breathed deeply . . . and felt nothing.

Disappointed, she sighed. Apathy wasn't what she expected.

Rocking her foot, she settled down and looked at Drew's closely cut hair, the defined muscles of his back, to a butt she not only enjoyed groping in the heat of passion, but now rested her legs against.

Another sigh escaped, and her eyes slid closed.

The tips of her fingers grazed his chest and connected with his heartbeat.

Her own heart galloped in response.

Shocked at the intensity of her reaction, Sydney took a mental step back and let her mind follow her body's lead.

Her first reaction had been to pull away, but she kept her fingertips against him.

A flow developed, and their bodies communicated without words, without sex, without expressions, without interference from the two people who'd be most affected by the outcome.

A sweet feeling of tenderness shimmered through her. But as the feeling blossomed, Sydney first felt, then accepted it.

This was love.

Her heart rejoiced, and she smiled.

Suddenly what started as an isolated feeling now attached to the man that lay asleep in front of her. He'd saved her life, and kept her alive, and protected her, and she loved him for it.

She moved her thigh to nudge him, but stopped.

She couldn't have it both ways. Even though she loved him, she couldn't let it go anywhere.

Sydney tucked her body into Drew's, and he stirred.

Now that she knew she was capable of loving, she knew she'd be responsible for breaking her own heart.

Sydney worked her arm free and was almost clear when Drew snagged her hand.

Her heartbeat spiked.

"Where are you going?"

She tried to shut off the emotions, afraid now that she'd recognized them, they'd show all over her face. But this love thing was like a waterfall. Free-flowing and relentless.

"It's time for work," she responded, glad she was behind him.

Turning, he was on his feet with her in his arms.

The bed had been warm and protecting. At room temperature, her skin filled with goose bumps.

"What are you doing?" she asked him.

"I need a shower."

"You have to go home."

He bumped her chin with his nose and then nipped at her. "Why?"

"I don't have a shower."

"Good. We can take a bath . . . and you can make sure all of my good parts are clean."

The innuendo made her G-spot contract. "I don't have time to play with you."

He about-faced. "Well, if this is all business, then let's just fuck and get it over with."

The bed where they'd spent hours enjoying themselves was so close. "Don't be crude."

"I'm sorry. An hour," he asked, tenderly. "It's all going to be there when we get back."

The poke of reality nearly broke the fantasy bubble they'd created.

Drew set her down, but Sydney wouldn't let him move farther away. He was right.

She reached for him. "Let's not waste time."

Drew sank his teeth into her shoulder. She yelped when he again lifted her in the air.

"I have things to do. Private things . . . in my bathroom."

Dawning hit him, and he set her down.

Sydney hurried into the private toilet room and took care of business, unwilling to let reality talk sense into what was an unreal situation. She began to fill the tub, then stopped at the sink and brushed her teeth, noticing the wet toothbrush that lay next to hers.

She entered the bedroom and didn't see Drew.

Had he regained his sanity and left? Insecurity lurked until she walked into the living room and saw him by the entertainment center, a photo album in his hands.

She cleared her throat. "Find anything interesting?"

He held the book out to her.

Once her hands closed around the cover, he lifted her in his arms and covered her breasts with his lips. "You when you were a little girl. You were beautiful then and still are."

He looked at her then, his gray-eyed gaze warming her to her toes. "Your mother was beautiful, too. You got your great looks and spirit from her."

How could he know that? Surely a few photos couldn't paint that clear a picture. Her gaze rested on the two shots that he'd been looking at.

Merry smiled at her, and Sydney hesitated, then smiled back.

She hadn't smiled at her mother in life for nearly twenty years. She didn't want to stop now.

Reading Merry's journals had painted a picture Sydney hadn't expected, but now respected. Merry, in her mind, had to leave in order to be free. Sydney, in a strange way, understood that need.

The heat kicked on, spreading warm air throughout the living room.

She let the photo album slide onto the table.

She'd make time to see all the pictures after she was finished with Drew.

"Let me down." Sydney tried to unwrap her legs from around his waist. "I don't want you to drop me."

"Trust me."

Drew held her tight as he carried her to the bathroom and lowered them both into the sunken Jacuzzi tub, facing each other.

He started the water, and it jetted around them in a swirl of bubbles.

Sydney looked at the man she now secretly loved and

struggled with the weakness and the power of her emotions.

Leaving him alone would be hard.

Drew caught her deep in thought. "Baby, don't start thinking. We are what we are, right?"

"Right."

"It's between us and no one else. And when it's done, it's done."

Before she could fully agree, he slid into her, and she welcomed him. The swirling water heightened her pleasure.

"After tonight, no more."

"I know," he said.

She drew her hands down his arms and back, his chest and then his face. As he rocked her world, Sydney kissed him, exploring pleasure and love simultaneously.

24

With only two days before the opening, Drew wondered when he'd sleep again. He watched the experienced waiters move through the paces of training and was glad things were going smoothly.

He'd expected to be harried with deliveries and last-minute snafus, but everything that had been thrown his way was dealt with quickly and efficiently. His new house manager had made the adjustment easier.

"Looks good, R.D."

"I'm glad." The distinguished, slightly graying man glanced up from his lists and nodded. He was of an indeterminate age, somewhere between thirty-five and sixty, but it didn't matter. He knew the restaurant business inside and out, and every restaurant he'd worked in for the past ten years would double his pay to have him back.

"The wine just arrived, so I'll oversee the inventory

and transfer into the cellar. You know, it's a good thing you don't have anything to do with Sydney Morris."

"Why do you say that?"

"There's a lot of support out there for you, man, a brotha tryin' to do the right thing. The radio spots are bangin', and it doesn't hurt that you brought me on board."

"We've had record cancellations," Drew reminded him. "I'm just trying to make sure we get through the first few months without going bankrupt."

"If you believed that, I wouldn't be here."

Drew realized his slight exaggeration had exposed a real insecurity. He didn't want anyone to know about him and Sydney.

"How about that wine delivery?"

"No problem, boss."

R.D. walked away, his hands around a secure two-way radio he used to communicate with the floor manager and assistant chef.

R.D. had surprised Drew and come over from a top Atlanta hotel, looking for something small and out of the rat race. He'd been looking for something new, and as he'd explained to Drew, he knew Satisfaction would be a challenge he was looking forward to leaving his mark on.

Besides, in the restaurant business, R.D. had the Midas touch.

Drew looked around. There was a lot working in his favor. And a lot against him. Having R.D. there wouldn't hurt.

Drew yanked his ringing cell phone off his waist. "Crawford."

"It's official," Mike said. "Sydney's going to get her license reinstated today. She'll be opening day after tomorrow on the fourteenth."

Drew heaved a sigh. After all they had been through, a small part of him still wanted FLIRTs doors to never open.

"So the church is giving up their fight?"

Mike made a strangled sound. "Lori King is one crafty attorney. She was going to shut their entire project down. I have to say, I'm never out of my league, but this time she outfoxed me."

"Those are not the words a man wants to hear from his attorney. What happened?"

"The church is going to sell the two feet of land they're over to the developer of the adjacent property. Then they're no longer within a mile of FLIRT."

Drew paced, stunned. Crawfords were rarely beat. Mike's admission was one for the annals of history. "You sound as if you admire the woman that will destroy me financially and cause you to lose a substantial investment."

"We're not going out like that. This could work, Drew. We just have to find a way."

"I'm all ears." Drew went to the window that faced FLIRT. Picketers marched in front of the store as news trucks and staff members fought to get inside.

During the past week, he'd seen Sydney only in short glimpses, and each time, his body reacted by wanting to be near her. He'd knocked on her door a couple nights ago, and when she didn't answer, he stopped knocking. She'd said it was over between them, and she'd meant it. That didn't stop him from missing her. But she was right.

"Have you talked to her about the lights shining into the restaurant?" Mike asked.

"No, but I will tonight."

"What's going on tonight?"

Drew flinched at his mess-up, having just made up his mind he had to see her. "Nothing. But I'll ask if I see her. I gotta go."

"Hey, man, I know you're disappointed, and I feel as if part of this is my fault. But this isn't the end of the rope. If they violate one ordinance, they're closed down for good."

Crowds of ministers and church folks paraded at the top of the hill. Their signs touted good businesses being sullied by the sin industry.

"Nobody is going to be able to get into either business if these picketers and news trucks are blocking the driveway and making everyone uncomfortable. Can you take care of that?"

"I'm on it," Mike said, sounding relieved to be doing something constructive. "Check on you later."

Drew referred to his list of things to do and called his cousin Trina. "Hey, what time is the crew coming over to set up for Lauren?"

"I know you're stressed, but I can't get a hello?"

Drew wiped his face. "Sorry, cuz. Hi, sweetheart, how are you?"

"Better now. I've been watching the news. How are you?"

"Feelin' like I should have my head examined. The parking lot is full of news people and picketers. Not exactly the crowd I was going for."

"Why not? Sell them some food, man. That's your business."

Drew laughed. Leave it to his cousin with the MBA to turn a negative into a money-making venture.

"You're probably right."

"I know I am. How are your deliveries? Did you get all your meat?"

"No, but I should be okay for the first two weeks. After that, I'll fly to Florida and meet with my suppliers."

"Two weeks? That's all the reserve you have? Are you kidding?"

"We cook everything fresh."

"That's a relative term. I don't think you're seeing the big picture."

Drew sat down, wishing Trina was here now. He'd show her the big picture. He had fresh meat, vegetables, desserts and chefs in the kitchens prepping so that when and if the crowds came, they'd be able to respond. He was as prepared as he could be.

"Trina, I've got this covered. Many of the reservations cancelled because of the store next door. I'm at about sixty percent for the first week. That's not great. I think we can handle the crowds."

"Of course, you're thinking small time. Obviously you need a great mind to help you out."

"Do I need to get a paring knife for your inflated ego?"

Trina laughed at her cousin. "No, but, because your daddy is one of my favorite uncles, I'll enlighten you. Got a pen ready?"

Drew crossed his ankles in front of him and stretched his arm across the back of the booth. "Shoot."

"Okay," she said. "You work next door to a famous dildo store where the owner has invited people in for her opening which coincides with yours. During that same interview that who knows, millions of people saw, she went on to say that she's eaten at Satisfaction, and it was good. Alone, the curious will stop by just to see what she was talking about—namely Aunt Roseanne's appetizers. Point two," Trina breathed, while he started feeling tightness in his chest.

"Yes, please enlighten me."

"Eight-time Grammy-winning artist Lauren Michaels is your cousin-in-law, and she's agreed to sing at the opening. World Congress Center, she sold out. What do you think will happen when people find out she's there tomorrow?"

"We didn't advertise."

"Shame on you!" Trina laughed, while Drew's trepidation grew to mammoth proportions. "My point is, big-headed cousin, if Lauren sells out the Dome, what do you think will happen with Satisfaction? By the way, sweetie, we put her appearance on our Web site."

Drew bit back a curse. "I've got to go."

Trina kept laughing. "I think you'd better. Before I forget, sound check at nine A.M. Thursday. And, we're traveling in our bus just so Lauren has someplace to change and we aren't a burden to you. Make sure there's adequate parking for the bus and two cars, fresh lemons and bottled spring water. In fact, I faxed over a list of our must haves. Did you have a chance to review it?"

Drew's head had started to throb. "I got it and left you a message that the stage is only big enough for the piano, which is being delivered today."

"You're not serious."

"Yes, I am."

"Give me the stage dimensions again."

"Eleven by fifteen."

"That's a freakin' closet!"

"You're exaggerating," Drew said calmly, agreeing silently.

"In a jail!"

"Hey now. We can work this out. This is a small restaurant with an intimate feel. Like a club, only better. I've seen Lauren in all settings. She showed out at this tiny theater in Paris. She's going to be able to do this."

"She's not India.Arie with just her voice and a guitar. Lauren needs space to do her thing. And the band," Trina huffed, having entered full panic mode. "Where will the band go?"

"We'll have room. Lauren on a high stool, a seriously scaled down band behind her. Think your sixteenth birthday basement party only better."

Trina laughed then, and Drew sighed in relief. They were going to be okay.

The door to Satisfaction blew open, and Sydney stomped in. His staff froze. The enemy had encroached upon the castle.

"Trina, I'll call you back."

"No, I'm calling you back. I have to clear all this with Lauren. I'm coming over tomorrow with my road and stage managers at seven in the morning to get a feel for the place myself. Later, cuz."

Drew closed his phone and stood. "Sydney."

"Drew. We have a problem."

"What's going on?" His gaze feasted on her. All he could think about was touching her. Talking to her. He missed that about as much as making love to her.

R.D. appeared from nowhere and motioned like a choir director, and the staff responded, going back to work.

R.D. gravitated near Drew, who passed him the list that had been written while Drew had talked to Trina.

R.D.'s eyebrows rose, and he directed two of the staff to remove the tables and chairs from the stage to ready it for the piano delivery.

"I was just informed that out-of-state protesters were called by someone in your camp. Is that true?"

"No."

She met his gaze evenly, then pulled a folded piece of paper from her pocket. "Can you deny this? It's from your family's company. They plan to block the driveway so that customers can't come to FLIRT."

"Sydney, think about it. I'd be hurting my business if I did something that stupid. The fax is fake. Someone's trying to create a situation where there isn't one."

She didn't speak. Didn't realize her power. Even though the staff moved around, Drew was aware that Sydney had a captive audience.

She pointed at his chest. "Fine, I believe you. Just don't ever lie to me."

He rocked her finger in his hand until she pulled it away. "Are we done here?" he asked.

Sydney looked out the window. "This has mushroomed into . . . ," she said, her voice full of awe. Then she looked at him and stood straighter.

"I thought it was against the law to block a private property."

"It is," he said, trying to act as natural as he wanted to feel. He'd spent nights here with Sydney, under the most extreme circumstances, and now in front of his staff, he couldn't act natural.

Drew didn't know what to make of his feelings. He'd hidden in plain sight for so long, maybe he didn't know that this was the equivalent to the emotional first base.

"I'm calling the cops," Sydney said, attempting to squeeze past Drew.

As if summoned by a force beyond their control, patrol cars edged onto the property, lights flashing, ordering the crowd to disperse.

Sydney peered out, squinting into the late afternoon sun.

"I already called them," he said softly.

She straightened, stepping back on one heel. She still looked like a warrior princess, but tame, like those times after they made love. "I owe you an apology," she said.

"I'll take a favor in return."

"What do you want?" she asked, her body language saying she was edging back toward her safety net of defensiveness.

For once Drew curtailed saying exactly what was on his mind. That he wanted a freak snow to overtake Atlanta tonight just so he could have a repeat performance of their time together. "The lights," he said. "The ones on this side of your store shine into the restaurant right onto the tables."

Sydney followed him to the spot in question and

peered out. She dialed her cell. "Chyna, turn on the lights on the west wall of the building."

The lights flickered and blazed, then began blinking.

Sydney flinched a little, and Drew hid his smile. "Not quite what my diners are expecting with their lobster tail."

"That might be a bit off-putting," she tentatively agreed. "What do you suggest?"

"I'm having privacy bushes installed in the spring. The ground's too hard right now. Until then, can we agree that during my dinner hours of four to ten, no lights?"

She folded her arms. "That's practically all night."

"Just on this side."

Outside, crowd control had been established, and the protesters moved off the sidewalk up to the street level. "Okay, deal."

As she backed away, he glimpsed a real smile around her mouth. "Have you eaten?" He didn't want her to leave, but he couldn't keep her here. The timing wasn't right.

"I could eat," she said noncommittally.

"I'll have something sent over. Anything else?"

She didn't look at him as she reached for the railing that led up the three steps. "Maybe . . ."

"What?" Drew followed, putting his arms behind his back.

"Perhaps tonight . . . we could compromise."

Wanting Sydney about crippled him. He locked his stance, accustomed to calling the shots. "Midnight."

"No," she said. "One."

"My place." Before she could comment, he walked away.

The remodeling of FLIRT had consumed the time between Merry's death and now, but as Sydney rested in the tub, she replayed every moment. There was nothing she'd have done again, except get to know her mother. She closed the final journal.

Merry had led an interesting life. Her only regret not seeing her daughter's face every day.

Sydney rested her head against the marble and greed. She'd missed that the most, too.

Merry was nothing like the woman Sydney had always thought her to be. Nothing like the woman her father had excommunicated from their lives.

Merry had been a kind woman. Had she been accepted as she was, she'd have had it all.

Sydney climbed out and dried off.

Going into the closet, she rifled through the clothes she'd brought over from her house and chose a sheer pink nightie that left little to the imagination.

After searching the bathroom for her lotion, Sydney stroked it on as she walked back into the bedroom.

At the dresser, she examined herself. Her body wasn't magazine perfect, but she wasn't bad either. In fact, she hadn't once heard Drew complain.

Smiling, she squeezed a little lotion into her palm to do her legs and feet, pulled open the second dresser drawer and blinked in surprise.

Laid out in the custom-built cabinet were vibrators and dildos of every size.

213

She pulled open the next drawer to find it filled t the rim with condoms of every size, shape and colo imaginable.

The next drawer was lined with a wide variety of cat-o nine-tails, and the next movies.

Sydney slid that one closed. Some things about Merr she didn't want to know. She examined the others an picked up her favorite toy of all. The Rabbit. Merry ha at least three of them in various versions and sizes.

Sydney smiled and gently put it back. She hadn died without pleasure.

She closed all the drawers except one, grabbed a fis ful of condoms, slipped her feet into her heels and le herself out of her apartment.

Knocking on Drew's door was risky. Her heart was in volved, and the last thing she wanted was for it to ge trampled under her need to be with the man she' fallen in love with.

Sydney realized the impracticality of her feelings but since she and Drew had a pact of sorts, expressin those feelings and getting them hurt wasn't an op tion.

She turned the handle, and the door slowly opened

The room was awash in candlelight, the music sof and sexy.

She walked inside, her feet sinking into the delicat suede of rose petals. She slipped off her heels and luxu riated in the feel.

She wanted everything about tonight to stay embla zoned in her memory. Including her response to thei lovemaking.

Their lives were about to change, and Sydney ha

he feeling neither of them would feel the same after
heir businesses opened.

"Drew," she called.

"Behind you. Don't turn around."

Under normal circumstances, Sydney didn't like tak-
ng orders from anyone, but the gentle instruction got
er juices flowing.

Drew grazed his lips along her shoulder.

"What are you doing?" she whispered.

"I'm going to make you feel."

"What?" The word rasped from her throat.

"Everything."

Nudging her into the center of the room, he eased
he thin strap down, his mouth claiming the flesh on
er back, leaving a wet trail. Sydney breathed through
er nose, trying to control her passion. Drew was play-
ng mind games with her. And with her body.

He knew what to do, but making love was a two-way
treet.

"When you're lying in bed, how do you like it?"

"What?" she asked.

"To be satisfied?"

His mouth captured her ear, and Sydney felt dizzy
om wanting him. Her resolve to stay strong crumbled.

"Tell me," he urged.

"With my legs open, my arms wide."

His knee slid between hers. "Spread 'em."

She stretched out her arms, and the condoms
ripped from her palm. Drew continued his tongue as-
ault on her back and up her left side, until he ducked
is head around and nipped her breast.

Sydney reached for him.

"Be still."

He held her arms out tight and resumed his down
ward sensual attack, when he bit her on her right cheel

She clenched, gasping, not realizing how sexy it wa
to have someone lavish attention on her ass. She kej
her arms out, her knees weakening when he connecte
with her warm wet folds.

Sydney sucked air between her teeth.

He held her up, his thumbs opening her.

"Drew, I won't last."

His tongue left her core, and her knees shook. "Kee
your arms out."

Sydney tried, but when his lips covered her clit,
powerful climax slammed into her. Coupled with th
sensation of falling and knowing he'd catch her, Sydne
didn't think she would ever feel this tremendous agair

Drew carried Sydney's trembling body to the couch
knowing he was ravishing her. He placed her on he
stomach against propped pillows, snagged one of th
condoms, tore it open and slid it on.

He lifted her, one hand on her jaw, and crushed he
mouth against his, while his other hand stroked her.

She squealed against his mouth, her body beginnin
what he now knew was the beginning of her ride to blis

Pushing her forward, he slid his fingers down he
back until he parted her folds and entered her.

Her body automatically bumped his, and he held he
arms back until the only thing she could concentrat
on was the feel of him moving inside of her.

"Come for me, baby," he said, and let her arms g
Following her forward against the pillows, he groun
into her, capturing her neck in his mouth.

Warm perspiration salted his lips, but he kept up his drive to the ultimate natural high.

Drew reached around and lavished her clit, and Sydney wailed, release tearing from her body.

Only then did Drew allow himself to join her on the magic carpet ride. Collapsing against her back, he sighed. "I love you, Sydney."

25

Sydney awakened to a February fourteenth with the sun shining and birds chirping. Traffic noise was at a minimum, and the protesters hadn't arrived yet to put a crimp in her day.

By all standards, the day was perfect.

Except she was mad as hell.

She showered and ate a quick breakfast, bracing herself, listening to hear if Drew was moving around next door. It was still early, but he might be up plotting ways to send her into another tailspin.

He loved her.

How dare he even go there?

Angrily she dropped her plate of toast into the sink and jumped when the china wobbled against the stainless steel. Drew had intentionally done this to her. Had he thought by confessing she'd fall head over heels and close her store? That wasn't going to happen.

Her secret love for him was one thing—she'd get over that—but after ravaging her, he had the audacity to confess an emotion that made her want to beat on him.

She'd had time to evaluate the appropriate response to his confession, after she'd fled his apartment. And she was sure that leaving him there, sweating, naked and confused, had been what he deserved.

She opened her front door quietly, walked down the hall and steps, her breath heaving out after she'd passed his door.

Drew didn't love her.

How could he when he couldn't tell anyone about her?

She was his best-kept secret. If Drew loved her so much, her owning FLIRT shouldn't be a problem.

If he loved her, he'd tell everyone, including his sympathetic protesters, and then maybe they'd leave her alone.

Sydney didn't see that happening.

She walked into FLIRT and flicked on the lights. The store had been transformed within the last three weeks. She searched for the word as she made coffee and set out refreshments.

FLIRT was sexy and tasteful.

The staff of five college-age ladies walked in led by Chyna. They fanned out, starting the sensual music Chyna had thought would set a sexy tone, turning on the flickering lights over the condom display and each girl moving to her zone. Chyna pulled Sydney aside, and her eyes misted.

"Dear, you've taken this place to a whole new level. I'm proud of you."

"Thanks, Chyna. Now, let's just keep our fingers crossed that we make money."

Chyna wiped her eyes. "The very first store your mother had, she said the same thing. But she was a smart businesswoman. She answered a need for women, and that's why this store is still here. We'll make money. The bigger question is whether it will be worth it in the end."

"What do you mean?" Sydney asked.

"By owning FLIRT, you give up your privacy, and you'll be targeted by all kinds of crazies. Merry had a stalker."

"She did?"

Sydney poured two cups of coffee, unable to resist this piece of information on Merry's life. "Did he try to harm her?"

"No, he adored her. He'd send flowers, candy, he'd call. Sometimes, he'd stand at the top of the hill and just watch."

"That sounds creepy."

"I know, but he claimed to love her."

"How did she feel about him? How did she feel about the attention?"

"She sold sex toys to the public, so when people tried to get in her business, she took it in stride. But Merry was very protective of you."

Chills ran up Sydney's spine. "What?"

"After your parents divorced, she tried to see you, but there were threats by some crazies, and they were targeting you. Pictures arrived of you leaving school one day, another of you playing in your yard, and one of you asleep."

"They broke into our house?"

Chyna nodded. "That scared Merry to death."

"Why weren't we aware of this?"

"She didn't want your father to be right. In some ways, I admired her, in others, I despised her, and we were best friends for years. I thought she should go home and be with you. But that life stifled her." Chyna smiled as Sydney's heart constricted. "She wanted you and she wanted to be free. Why do you think she gave you her store?"

Sydney had never understood Merry, until now. On the eve of opening her sex-toy shop, Sydney felt her heart lift with love for the mother she'd hardly known. Merry had given her freedom, and with it, her love.

"Sydney," Amber called from the front door. "The protesters have begun to arrive. Should we take them some coffee?"

Chyna gave her a curious look. "No, honey. We aren't feeding the enemy. If they buy something, they can have coffee. Come on, ladies. Gather round."

Syd waited for the associates to gather by the cash register. "We're in for a big day. The media will be here, customers, and of course, the people who don't want us here. It's going to be a long day, but if you ever feel like you can't handle someone, or if you need a break, I'll be right here with you."

"Me, too," Chyna said. "I'll be helping on the floor until we close tonight."

"That's right. Remember to give everyone free condoms and"—Sydney shrugged—"have fun."

A knock sounded on the door, and everyone turned

to look. Sydney rubbed her hands together. "It's time. Go ahead, Gail," she said to a petite woman who wore her hair in tasteful dreads. "Let's open."

Gail hurried over and looked out, then turned back, her mouth gaping in surprise. "You are not going to believe who this is."

"You're right," Chyna agreed, "until you open the door and let them in."

If Gail's golden brown face could have reddened, it would have. "Right," she whispered and opened the door.

Sydney waited with a mixture of trepidation and curiosity. She felt Gail's shock when in walked singing diva Lauren Michaels, a tall, leggy woman, along with Asia, Africa and Europe, the women who'd rescued her from her house.

"Asia, I mean Jade!" Sydney exclaimed. "Wow. What a surprise."

The women burst out laughing, moving as a group toward Sydney.

"That's not usually the response we get," Jade explained. "People always fall over Lauren first."

"Goodness! Ms. Michaels. I'd know you anywhere. How are you?"

"Fine. This is my daughter, Shayla, and my cousins, Trina and Tracy."

"Africa and Europe. You're all related." Dawning hit as the resemblance knocked Sydney in the chest. "You're all Crawfords. Drew's relatives."

Sydney took a step back, and they all reached for her.

"She's going down, get a chair," Jade ordered.

For a moment Sydney felt her head go light, then a

gaggle of words float around her. She looked up at the women surrounding her, gray eyes swimming every where, and she closed her own.

"Just breathe, sweetie, this family is quite overwhelm ing," Lauren reassured her. "Jade and I are the only normal ones."

Sydney grunted her laughter, and Lauren took her hand while Jade pushed everyone back. "I'd say we should give her some room."

"I'm good," Sydney managed. She nodded her thanks for the cup of water and sipped. "Um . . . why are you here?"

"We came to shop," Lauren said gently. "Any woman who can send the Crawford men into a summit meet ing, I had to meet."

She looked between the five women. "What's a sum mit meeting?"

They all laughed. Their smiles were even similar.

"It's a family meeting the men have when they're con fused," Lauren said with such innocence, Sydney knew there was probably a hilarious story behind her smile. "We don't have much time, so do you mind if we get our shopping out of the way before the crowd hits?"

Surprise filled her. "Sure," she said, but a question lingered. "I read that you were married."

"Happily." Lauren grinned, pivoting on impossibl high heels. "But I like to keep things fresh, if you know what I mean."

Shayla, Lauren's daughter, covered her mouth before yanking on Lauren's arm. "I might be married, but I still don't want to know about my mother and father having sex. Mom, let's shop on opposite sides of the store."

"Ten minutes," Jade announced, setting her watch as she'd done at Sydney's house. "We still have a sound check to prepare for."

The sales associates had moved back to their zones, but buzzed with excitement. Lauren Michaels was in the house!

Chyna stood at the counter beside Sydney. "We're going to be a huge hit," she expressed quietly.

"I sincerely hope so. I'll stay up here. You go on the floor and do your thing."

Chyna bustled from behind the counter, offering the ladies shopping baskets. She passed them to the sales associates and told them to keep them on their arms while they helped the customers shop.

Eight minutes later, the women stood at the counter, talking and comparing as Sydney rang up their orders. "Do you mind me asking how far you have to travel for your sound check?"

"Next door. I'm performing tonight."

The register beeped after Sydney hit too many buttons at once. "At Satisfaction?"

"Yes, are you coming by?"

"That's three hundred forty-seven dollars. I didn't know you were going to be there. But probably not. The owner and I aren't exactly friends." *We screw around, and he said he loved me, but that's all.*

A look passed between the women that ended in smirky smiles. "You all look so much alike, even you two," Sydney said to Jade and Lauren, although she knew they'd married into the clan.

"Four-eighteen," she said to Jade, who'd bought a

whip. "It's for my mother, don't ask." The Crawford women all sighed.

"Once you marry a Crawford, you take on characteristics that eventually seal your fate as one of them," Jade explained, although Sydney didn't feel any smarter for knowing.

"I have no idea what you're talking about."

"It's a family thing. You'll figure it out one day." Sydney didn't want to express any further confusion at the bizarre prediction. Her head was swimming with too much information and too many questions. If she were speaking to Drew, she would ask him. But she wasn't, so she couldn't.

Trina and Tracy put their orders together, each buying the special vibrator of the week. "Hey," Trina said, defending their purchases when Shayla tsked. "We don't have men. I've got to get some satisfaction somewhere. How are we on time, Jade?"

"Maxxed out. Let's roll."

Lauren took Sydney's hand. "Please come over tonight at ten as my special guest. I have a reserved table and no one to sit at it."

"What about your family?"

The women behind her laughed. "We don't get to watch shows anymore," Shayla filled in. "She's got us working."

Lauren winked at her daughter. "If she gave me some grandbabies, she wouldn't be working. Sydney, I'd like to invite you and your entire staff over as my guests."

All six of her staff members' heads bobbed up and down like bobblehead dolls. How could she refuse? "Okay. Ten it is."

"Thanks. See you tonight." The group of women chattered as they left the store. After the bell rang over the door, four seconds of silence passed before all the girls started screaming and laughing. Sydney couldn't help but join in.

Lauren Michaels, the most famous R&B singer in the country, had just bought body gels and sexy lingerie at her store, and had invited them to a concert.

Sydney glanced at the register tape, then showed it to Chyna, who'd shooed the girls back to their zones. "They spent over two thousand dollars in ten minutes. That's our daily goal."

Chyna patted her hand. "Every day won't be this way, but success is yours, claim it."

Gail opened the door, and women poured in, their squeals excited as they spread throughout the store.

It was showtime.

"Thanks, Chyna," Sydney said, moving from behind the counter. "Welcome to FLIRT." She greeted a shy, light-skinned woman. "How can I help you?"

"I want something that will stimulate me while my husband and I make love."

Sydney walked her over to the wall she'd personally stocked and handed her two different types of bullet vibrators. "These," she said, her stomach getting a bit nervous, "worked for me."

The woman looked grateful. "Thanks."

The door chimed, and more customers flowed in. Three of the five looked like some of the protesters, but Sydney wasn't sure. She didn't want to keep them out unless they started trouble.

Chyna stayed on them, making suggestions all the way until the time they left the store. Only one of them bought a magazine on sexy lingerie.

By the end of the night, Sydney was bone tired but thrilled. Sales for the day had been exceptional, and if they kept it up, she'd be nearly a millionaire by fall.

Drew's last offer floated through her mind, and she wondered how his restaurant had done today.

Her heart fluttered, and she sighed as she refilled body gels, a top seller of the day.

"Can we go to see Lauren Michaels," Amber asked, already slipping on her leather jacket and purse.

"Sure. Thanks for a great effort today, ladies. See you tomorrow."

"You're not coming?"

"Somebody needs to restock."

They all had guilty looks on their faces. "If you want, I'll stay," Gail offered, clearly disappointed.

Sydney escorted them to the door. "I wouldn't make you pass this up for anything. Besides, I want you back on time tomorrow. Have fun."

"Try to come, okay?" Chyna said, wrapping her neck in a vibrant purple scarf.

Sydney nodded. "I'll try."

The ladies poured out the door, waving goodbye.

Locking up, she walked to the back, grabbed her cart and filled it with boxes of merchandise, when an eager knock rattled the door.

She hurried over. "Who forgot something?"

Opening it, she was stunned to see one of the men who'd been a protester from the very beginning. "We're closed." Sydney tried to slam the door, but he wedged himself inside the frame.

"Nastiness begets nastiness," he said, and threw a half-filled bucket of roaches on her.

She stumbled to the floor, screaming.

26

Drew and R.D. rolled a table behind the restaurant, taking it to the storage unit.

"I heard screaming." R.D. looked around the back lot, but saw no one.

Drew was halfway to the back door of FLIRT. "Get Nick and Jade. Tell them to take the front."

Drew ran, using the key he'd realized a month ago was to FLIRT's back door. A crash sounded, and Sydney screamed again as a crazed man pulled down one shelf after another on and around her. She'd managed to get to the end of a row, but she was still in danger.

She looked as if she was fighting with herself until Drew saw bugs crawling all over her. By her collar he pulled her from the debris, and she fought harder. "Syd, stop," he ordered, but she didn't, hysterical.

The man turned toward the male voice, and a feral grin parted his face.

"I'm helping you," he said, yanking down more shelves.

Drew got up and tackled him, not giving him time to prepare for a fight. They rolled around, his strength surprising Drew, who knew after this fight, he'd be in the gym.

Finally he landed a good series of punches, and the man fell face first onto the floor. Jade, Nick and Keisha burst through the door.

The women immediately went to Sydney, who was now facedown, shaking violently.

As soon as they touched her, she stiffened, then went still.

"She'll be out for a minute," Nick announced, taking in the debris and the reason for her reaction. There were roaches crawling everywhere.

"Jade," the Marine Corps Colonel said to his wife, "stay down here with her in case she wakes up. Keisha, call the police and then get Chaz and the rest of the kids. They can help clean up, but first this place needs to be exterminated."

Drew came from the back with duct tape and subdued the unconscious man. He was winded, but filled with adrenaline.

"Damnit. Why was she here by herself?"

"Lauren invited everyone over for the concert. She must have stayed behind to restock the shelves. Her cart is over there."

"Let's get her up," Drew said. "She won't like being on the floor."

"We don't know how badly she's hurt." Jade thrust er arm out, stopping him. Her hands trembled, and Nick gripped his wife's hands. "I hate bugs, what can I ell you?"

Jade had been shot, and he'd never seen her flinch ntil now. Everyone had their weakness.

Drew's was Sydney.

Nick had his phone to his ear. "Eric, we need you ext door at FLIRT. We've got the owner Sydney Morris nconscious."

Keisha came from the back room with bug spray for nts. "You think this will work?"

Drew shrugged, his body twitching from the action. Go for it."

Eric burst through the door. "What happened?"

"One crazy man, Drew beat unconscious, and Sydney, he newest inductee into the Crawford family," Jade said.

Eric got on all fours and peered at Sydney's uncon-cious body. He asked a series of questions to determine er injuries. "She was conscious when you arrived?"

"Fighting to get the bugs off her, but conscious."

"Drew, Jade, step back. Let's gently roll her. Nick, ght to left."

They flipped Sydney, and Jade moaned. Dead bugs overed her torso, face and hands.

"She's going to be one upset lady when she wakes ," Eric said, pushing her hair from her face. "Nick, ll Lauren. I need the bag from the bus."

"I'll get it, Eric. I need some air," Jade said, looking ghtly green. "Besides, Lauren will be going on in ten inutes."

He handed her his keys. "Kenny's driving tonigh
Tell him the bag is in the locked cabinet under th
sink."

Drew kneeled down beside his cousin. "Do you thin
it's safe to move her upstairs?"

"What's up there?" Keisha asked, standing the emp
can on one of the only undisturbed shelves. The plac
reeked of pesticide.

"Sydney has an apartment next door to mine. Hers
number two." Drew hurried in the back of FLIR
dumped her purse and returned with her keys.

Eric finished a preliminary examination, but shoo
his head. "I want her to come to before we conside
moving her. It's Sydney, right?"

"Right."

Eric cleaned all the dead bugs off her face wit
Nick and Keisha completing the task of her lower hal
Eric gently shook her shoulders. "Sydney, wake u
Sydney."

They held their collective breath, when she moane
in a high-pitched squeal. "Sydney, you're okay. Ope
your eyes."

She jerked her head, her hands flailing. "Bugs," sl
groaned.

"They're all gone. We got them," Eric reassure
her.

Drew held back, watching Sydney come to. He didr
know what to do. This was completely out of his leagu

The police walked in, led by Jade, who directed the
to the perpetrator. Drew moved toward them, being tl

only witness who could give an accurate account of what happened.

The man was conscious, quietly watching the action. The police cut the tape off and then dragged him to his feet. "She shouldn't have brought perversion to our community. We were trying to help you."

"I don't need your help," Drew shot back.

"I saw the way you looked at her. Say you don't want her here, and we'll keep hammering away until she breaks. Say nothing, and we'll make sure you go down with her."

Drew felt the stare of everyone in the place, except Eric, who continued to talk to Sydney.

Drew didn't know what to say. He'd sunk nearly every dime he had into Satisfaction.

The officers looked at him and then led the perpetrator out the door. He closed the door behind them and walked back over. Sydney was trying to sit up. The look she gave Drew could cut steel, but she didn't say a word as she gave up and lay on the floor.

"Who are you?" she asked Eric.

"Dr. Eric Crawford. This is my brother Nick."

"Ma'am," Nick greeted softly. "This is my sister-in-law Leisha and my wife Jade."

"You're all Crawfords?"

"Yes," Eric said, smiling. "That's not so good for us today, huh?"

"Not today," she said, biting her lip to keep from crying. "I'm grateful for your help."

"Does anything hurt?"

"Can you come a little closer?"

Nick and Eric bent over her, and she whispered to them. Eric gingerly checked her right arm, and she winced.

Drew paced, unable to reason with himself why he hadn't told that man to go to hell.

In a low voice Eric spoke to Sydney, but Drew saw tears streak from her eyes and land on the carpet.

He moved forward, only to be stopped by Keisha's warning hand. There was mention of a hospital, but he saw Sydney shake her head.

Eric spoke again, and Sydney reluctantly nodded.

"We're going to help you stand," Eric instructed, "but I want you to get your bearings before we get you up to your apartment. Lean on Nick."

"How do you know where I live?" Sydney asked.

"Drew told us. Jade," he said, and she got down next to him, listened, then stood.

"I'll carry her up," Drew offered, but got no response from anyone. It was as if he hadn't spoken.

Nick and Eric braced Sydney on both sides and eased her onto her feet.

Nick leaned down and talked to Sydney, then called Jade over again. The two women conferenced, and then Jade came back to Drew. "We need to borrow your apartment."

"What the hell is going on?"

"She wants to shower before going to the hospital to have her arm x-rayed. May we have the keys, cuz?"

Nick had already lifted Sydney and was in the middle

236

of the Crawford caravan heading to the back of the store. Drew handed them over, feeling helpless. "Let me do something."

"She doesn't want your help. She said that specifically. I'll call you." Jade gave him a sympathetic look and hurried ahead of the group of his family as they cared for Sydney.

27

"You have to let it go, Syd. Forgive your father or move on. You can't be bitter. How many reps have you done now?"

"I'm not, Evette Elizabeth. And I just completed the second set of fifteen." Sydney held the five-pound dumbbell in her right hand and lowered it to the floor.

"A broken arm sure hasn't stopped you. Nothing does anymore."

"I'm glad it's healed, too. The physical therapist said I could do weights now. I just don't like that this arm is bigger than my left."

"What about your father?"

"He still won't speak to me. But when I called him yesterday, he didn't hang up. I talked and he listened. I told him about the diaries and the letters I'd found that Terry had written to me that he'd returned."

"I still can't believe that. You could have had a relation ship with her all that time."

"It's a hard reality to accept. I'm still struggling wit it. All that time I thought she didn't love me. I w; wrong."

"No, you were misled. But I don't want you to carr the sins of the past into your new life. You're so health and whole. I'm proud of you," Evette said.

"Thanks. I left the door open for him. My father h; to take the next step. Now, can we move on to a happie topic? Namely you and Mr. Fireman. How's it going?"

"He's divorced now and living on his own for th first time since college. I think that freaked him out bit."

Sydney laughed, stowing her basket of weights ne> to her punching bag. She hadn't used it in months. ' can imagine."

"We were in the linen store last week, and he didn know what kind of sheets he wanted. He didn't kno anything about thread count or comforters. After h got over the initial shock of there being so many, he l; on every thread count in the store. It was hilarious."

Sydney laughed, the feeling transforming her bod She hadn't laughed nearly enough. "Evette?"

"Yeah?"

"What about you two? How's that going? You were s serious for a minute, and now it seems like you're be friends, but not lovers."

"I know, but let me put your fears to rest. We get it o regularly, but our relationship has transformed. He got to find himself, and I don't want to be a remnant i his post-divorce life, so we're taking it very slow."

"You sound so healthy," Sydney marveled.

Evette laughed. "Don't let what sounds good fool you. I've had my bad nights when I've dialed nine digits of his phone number and made myself not finish the rest because I knew getting with him when I was needy wouldn't help him or me."

"Why, 'Vette? I needed help, and boy, did I get it."

"You mean from the Crawfords?"

" 'Vette, I swear, it's like a colony of gray-eyed men who called me ma'am and carried me to my apartment. Women who helped me pick dead bugs from my hair and shower. I was pathetic. My arm was fractured, and my heart was broken. They still come by my store and are so sweet to me."

"Why do you think you don't deserve people doing nice things for you?"

"I'm not sure—I'm lying." Sydney stopped herself. "I was emotionally empty before I met Drew, and he gave me something to hold on to. I gave him all of me, Evette. I blossomed by falling in love with him."

"You could still have that. But you'd have to forgive his lapse in judgment."

"He didn't stand up for me. I felt abandoned, 'Vette. I never want to feel that way again."

"Drew is only a man. He made one mistake in a sea of things that he did right. Come on, Syd. Everybody makes mistakes, and he can't be held responsible for the sins of the past. And he can't atone for the sins of your father."

Sydney felt as if she'd been struck with a lightning bolt. Of course 'Vette was right: "I don't know what to say to him. I've always had a hard time fixing things.

241

No, I'm just going to leave it alone. There'll be others, 'Vette. I'll fall in love again."

"Oh, Syd. I wish you wouldn't give up."

"I don't know what else to do except move on with my life. I've got the store. I should be happy."

"Just think about it, okay?"

"If I see Drew, I'll try."

"Good," 'Vette said, the lack of enthusiasm in her voice a dead giveaway that she didn't believe Sydney. But Sydney couldn't help that. She and Drew were over. And now that she'd achieved all that she wanted, she had to come to grips with the fact that money and happiness weren't synonymous.

28

Nearly six months had passed since Drew had spoken to Sydney, and he couldn't say that he'd ever known that time could pass so slowly. Summer had hit with a vengeance, bringing to Satisfaction an urban, eclectic, artsy crowd.

His business had suffered, but not the way he'd thought it would.

This crowd didn't eat red meat, but expensive fish and exotic appetizers that Drew was only too happy to provide. They loved the family favorites, and he'd changed the menu and added most of his mother's delicacies.

He'd added entertainment to the dinner hour and had the privacy bushes planted this past spring.

But that hadn't mattered. His customers didn't care that there was a sex store next door. It wasn't unusual for him to see little pink bags with FLIRT emblazoned in gold across the front on the tables in his restaurant.

Connor Smith, the man who'd vandalized Sydney's store and broken her arm, had pleaded guilty to felony assault and criminal trespass and had been sentenced to jail.

Drew had tried to connect with Sydney many times over the months, but she wouldn't have any of it. She'd sold her house, he heard from a reporter who wanted to interview her, but Drew also knew she wasn't living in her mother's apartment anymore.

Occasionally he thought he heard her, but he'd wait at his door, and she'd never pass by.

Often his female cousins came into Satisfaction with little bags from FLIRT, but they never discussed their friendship with Sydney.

Drew had been completely and utterly shut out of her life. He'd never been lonelier.

R.D. walked over with a piece of paper in his hand. "Boss man, let's talk."

Drew snapped out of his fog and gestured his friend into the seat. "What's on your mind?"

"It's time for me to go."

"R.D., we talked about this when you came on. You have a two-year contract."

"I know, but you're successful already. You don't need me."

"We're successful because we work together. Now, what's really the problem?"

"I've met someone."

Drew shifted in his seat. "Who is she?"

"Lori King. The attorney that represented FLIRT against Satisfaction. We're in love."

"Oh. Okay. When the hell did that happen?"

"During the past six months that you've been in a fog working and not thinking about whatever you've been thinking about. In case you hadn't noticed, we've struck gold. But you don't need me anymore, so I need to move on. My lady and I want to take some time off and travel."

"You get time off. Why do you have to quit?"

R.D. smiled. "I didn't think you'd be cool with me dating the woman who beat the Crawfords. And knowing that Sydney is closing FLIRT, you got what you wanted. You can expand—"

"Whoa, back up. Sydney's closing FLIRT?"

R.D. covered his mouth. "I can't believe you didn't know. That's what you wanted, right?"

"Yeah," Drew said, standing. "That's what I wanted."

"Apparently she got what she wanted, but she said something about it not being what she wanted, and now she has to leave some things behind."

"Where's she going?"

"She's gone."

"Where, R.D.?"

"Brazil and then Lori said something about her going to France. Her mother always wanted her to see France."

A myriad of emotions crashed into Drew, who grabbed his briefcase. He started away, then turned back to R.D. "You're not quitting, because you've been promoted to acting manager. I'll be back."

"When?"

"I don't know. However long it takes. Take care of my shop."

Drew hurried home, grabbed his passport and left his apartment.

* * *

Sydney sat in the window seat and sank into the leather. She'd flown before, but never first class. She palmed the locket around her neck, the last of Merry's diaries on her lap. Sydney had read twenty years' worth, and the one thing she'd come away with was that Merry had loved her dearly.

She turned toward the window, holding the diary.

We're taking our first trip together. Just us, Mom.

The empty seat next to Sydney was symbolic, but she wished it were filled.

She wished Drew were with her, but she shut off the thought.

After six months, didn't love die?

She gazed out the window, the tears welling again. She should be over him.

Soon he'd learn that she'd granted his wish. FLIRT would close its doors, and his restaurant would flourish. He was successful now, she knew that. But he'd absolutely blossom without the taint of her business next to his.

"What can I get you to drink, Ms. Morris?"

"Sweet tea," she ordered, forgetting she was in New York City and not Georgia. She smiled apologetically at the flight attendant. "I'm sorry, just water. I plan on sleeping the whole way there."

The attendant returned with her water.

"How soon before we take off?"

"About fifteen minutes. We have a few late arriving passengers and are standing by for them. Is this your first time abroad?"

"Yes."

"Well, enjoy. I got word that the flight is overbooked. If we need this seat, you'll be given a complimentary ticket to use at another time."

Sydney smiled. "No problem. It was more symbolic than anything."

The attendant gave her a questioning look, but Sydney waved her off. "It's nothing. Please, if someone needs the seat, they're welcome to it."

"Thank you. Here's a complimentary sleep mask for your eyes. Excuse me, I've got to board the passengers."

Sydney slid the mask in place and got comfortable. If she slept most of the way, she'd be fresh for Brazil. She breathed deeply, then settled down. Soon she'd be asleep.

"Welcome," the attendant greeted a passenger who brought a hurried air with him. He settled a bag next to Sydney, and she scooted over.

"Water," he whispered to the attendant, then sat down. The plane taxied and floated into the sky, and as hard as Sydney tried to relax, she couldn't fall asleep.

Mainly because the man next to her wore cologne that reminded her of Drew. At one point she peeked out of the sleep mask, but he'd gone to the rest room, so she covered her eyes and settled her neck against her pillow. She felt him come back and sit down.

"May I disturb you a moment?" the man asked her quietly.

Sydney sat up and prepared to remove the mask. "You don't have to do that," he said, taking her hand. "I just wanted your opinion on something. I did someone I love wrong, and for months I haven't known how to apologize. Now she's selling her business and leaving. I took a chance and followed her, hoping she'd forgive me and . . . "

"Forgive you?" she asked, a lump in her throat.

"I want her to come home."

"Is that your best offer?"

"Besides the most sincere apology a man ever had to give, I'd shower her with love and food. I'm a chef, and I'd never turn my back on her again."

"You betrayed her?"

"I didn't acknowledge my feelings for her at a crucial time, and I should have."

"I bet that tore her up. But maybe she was already dealing with rejection from her father and lumped everything into a big ball and took it out on the only other important man in her life."

"Maybe," he said. "But for my part, I'm sorry."

"I think she might be sorry, too, but she didn't know how to apologize. Is that your best offer?"

"I'd offered her a half million dollars."

"And?"

"If she wanted it, I'd give it to her, but she'd have to marry me and love me forever and have my children, and keep her sex-toy store open. You see, I love her, and I want her to be my wife. I even bought her a ring." He quieted. "What do you think she'd say if I told her all of this?"

Sydney couldn't speak. She tried to pull the mask off, but it was stuck to her skin by her tears.

Drew gently pulled it away from her face, leaving it around her neck, and she got her first good look at him in six months.

He was bronzed and more fit than she'd ever seen

him. She missed looking at him. Talking to him. Making love to him. She missed all of those things and so much more.

She reached for his hand.

"If you were her," he said, "what would you say?"

"What's her name?" she whispered as he pressed his lips into her temple.

"Sydney Merry Morris."

"I'd say she probably doesn't want your money."

"And?"

"That she loves you and would definitely accept your apology only if you accepted hers."

He picked up her hand and kissed it. "Done. What if I don't want her to sell her business? I think the way I use her sex toys on her is kind of sexy."

She smiled through her tears. "Maybe she could promote her most loyal employee and let her run things for a while. Maybe then your lady friend could concentrate on you."

"What about the ring?" he asked, so softly her heart nearly broke.

"That would take some convincing," she said, looking into his eyes. "What if she wanted to travel? What if he wasn't interested in doing that? She'd be stuck in love with a man who didn't share her dreams."

Drew slid up the arm between their seats and kissed her long and slow.

"What if he semi-retired from his business and part of his dream is to travel the world with the woman he loves? What if he wanted to know if she would marry him?"

Love for Drew and her life encompassed Sydney.

Sydney quietly thanked Merry for FLIRT and for bringing her to Drew.

Sydney kissed him, glad that her life was now whole. She cupped Drew's face. "I believe she'd say yes. I know I would."

Dear Readers,

Thank you so much for enjoying the latest Crawford story *FLIRT*. Many of you have been with me from the very beginning of this family back when *Silken Love* first hit the stores in 1997. Over the years there've been so many times when I thought, *surely they don't want another Crawford story*, but it was inevitable, someone would write to me and ask me for more.

I love this family. They're supportive, good, loving people everybody can identify with. They represent the good in us and the good we want in our lives. I'm proud that God blessed me with the ability to create, and I hope my stories give you hours of pleasure, too. If you haven't already read the entire family, enjoy *Silken Love; Keeping Secrets; Endless Love; Doctor, Doctor; Kissed* and *Flirt*.

Be sure to check out my website at *www.authorcarme green.com* for the latest news on the Crawford's and see the Crawford family tree. I'll be running contests about this wonderful family, so get the books, check the site, and leave me a note. You could win prizes. Or you may e-mail me at *carmengreen1201@yahoo.com*. Also, stay tuned for my next novel from Kensington/Dafina Books, *What a Fool Believes*. You're guaranteed to laugh and have a good time.

Thank you for your support, and happy reading!

Blessings,

Carmen

Check Out These Other
Dafina Novels

Sister Got Game
0-7582-0856-1

by Leslie Esdaile
$6.99US/**$9.99**CAN

Say Yes
0-7582-0853-7

by Donna Hill
$6.99US/**$9.99**CAN

In My Dreams
0-7582-0868-5

by Monica Jackson
$6.99US/**$9.99**CAN

True Lies
0-7582-0027-7

by Margaret Johnson-Hodge
$6.99US/**$9.99**CAN

Testimony
0-7582-0637-2

by Felicia Mason
$6.99US/**$9.99**CAN

Emotions
0-7582-0636-4

by Timmothy McCann
$6.99US/**$9.99**CAN

The Upper Room
0-7582-0889-8

by Mary Monroe
$6.99US/**$9.99**CAN

Got A Man
0-7582-0242-3

by Daaimah S. Poole
$6.99US/**$8.99**CAN

Available Wherever Books Are Sold!

Check out our website at www.kensingtonbooks.com.

Look For These Other
Dafina Novels

If I Could
0-7582-0131-1

by Donna Hill
$6.99US/**$9.99**CAN

Thunderland
0-7582-0247-4

by Brandon Massey
$6.99US/**$9.99**CAN

June In Winter
0-7582-0375-6

by Pat Phillips
$6.99US/**$9.99**CAN

Yo Yo Love
0-7582-0239-3

by Daaimah S. Poole
$6.99US/**$9.99**CAN

When Twilight Comes
0-7582-0033-1

by Gwynne Forster
$6.99US/**$9.99**CAN

It's A Thin Line
0-7582-0354-3

by Kimberla Lawson Roby
$6.99US/**$9.99**CAN

Perfect Timing
0-7582-0029-3

by Brenda Jackson
$6.99US/**$9.99**CAN

Never Again Once More
0-7582-0021-8

by Mary B. Morrison
$6.99US/**$8.99**CAN

Available Wherever Books Are Sold!

Check out our website at www.kensingtonbooks.com.

Grab These Other
Dafina Novels
(mass market editions)

Grab These Other
Dafina Novels
(trade paperback editions)

Grab These Other
Thought Provoking Books

Adam by Adam
0-7582-0195-8

by Adam Clayton Powell, Jr
$15.00US/$21.00CAN

African American Firsts
0-7582-0243-1

by Joan Potter
$15.00US/$21.00CAN

African-American Pride
0-8065-2498-7

by Lakisha Martin
$15.95US/$21.95CAN

The African-American Soldier
0-8065-2049-3

by Michael Lee Lanning
$16.95US/$24.95CAN

African Proverbs and Wisdom
0-7582-0298-9

by Julia Stewart
$12.00US/$17.00CAN

Al on America
0-7582-0351-9

by Rev. Al Sharpton
with Karen Hunter
$16.00US/$23.00CAN

Available Wherever Books Are Sold!

Visit our website at **www.kensingtonbooks.com**